'Fabulous fairies

Guardian, Best New Children's Books, Summer 2015

'The craziest and funniest book I've read in ages'
Andy Stanton, author of the Mr Gum *series*

'I couldn't put this book down and will
recommend it to all my friends'
Evie, age 8, for lovereading4kids.co.uk

'Silly spells, delectable dresses, magical mishaps
and ridiculous riddles, this is a witch story like no
other – and it's a blast!'
Bookseller

'I'm a big fan of the main fairy'
Fran the Fabulous Fairy

'Fizzing with fun'
Daily Mail

Also by Sibéal Pounder

WITCH GLITCH

SIBÉAL POUNDER

Illustrated by
Laura Ellen
Anderson

BLOOMSBURY
LONDON OXFORD NEW YORK NEW DELHI SYDNEY

Bloomsbury Publishing, London, Oxford, New York, New Delhi and Sydney

First published in Great Britain in October 2016 by Bloomsbury Publishing Plc
50 Bedford Square, London WC1B 3DP

www.bloomsbury.com

BLOOMSBURY is a registered trademark of Bloomsbury Publishing Plc

A CIP catalogue record for this book is available from the British Library

ISBN 978 1 4088 8034 0

Typeset by RefineCatch Limited, Bungay, Suffolk
Printed and bound in Great Britain by CPI Group (UK) Ltd, Croydon CR0 4YY

1 3 5 7 9 10 8 6 4 2

The Story So Far

Last time in Ritzy City:

Deep down below the sink pipes in the witchy world of Sinkville, Celia Crayfish, the most evil witch to ever rule the place, RETURNED, and it was terrifying. Good witches battled evil ones, along with a lot of fairies in specially designed hats. Tiga and her fellow Witch Wars witches saved the day and banished Celia Crayfish and all the other evil witches to a cheese factory above the pipes. That was dreadful for all of them, apart from Miss Heks — because she loves only one thing in life. And that one thing is cheese.

Tiga also found her long-lost mum, Gretal Green! It turned out she had been sucked

into her hat during the Big Exit (long story . . .), along with all the other witches in Silver City. So, evil witches banished, and the witches of Silver City saved, Tiga jumped on a hoover (don't ask) with her mum and her slug (who she discovered is called Sluggfrey) and off they went to Silver City to live happily ever after . . .

Oh, and Fran joined them, too. When we left them, Fran was suggesting they all sing a song. She was in the process of trying to relaunch her singing career. In the olden days Fran had been in a band called Just Fran, which included her and two other fairies – Crispy and Millbug-Mae. Fran shouted self-centred lyrics while Crispy clapped next to her. Millbug-Mae did absolutely nothing.

Anyway, on that perfectly crisp evening, Tiga, her mum and Sluggfrey soared through the clouds to the sound of Fran singing her first and what she herself calls best song ever written, 'Fran, Fran, For Ever'.

It looked like they were zooming towards a happily ever after. But things are never that simple, are they?

A New Life in Silver City (Also Dennis)

*Has there been anyone
more fabulous, ever?
Nopedy nope!
Fran, Fran, for ever!*

'I'm never going to get that song out of my head,' Tiga groaned. 'And I haven't seen Fran for *weeks*.'

'It really sticks, doesn't it? I woke up singing it,' Gretal Green said as she poured a silvery liquid into a tiny teapot. It was being held in the middle of the table by a lean arm clad in a beautiful lace glove.

'Is that … a real witch's arm in that glove?' Tiga asked, wincing as it swivelled to face her.

Ever since she'd arrived in Silver City, Tiga had

had so many questions, like why did everyone foot-wave instead of hand-wave when saying hello? Why did Winglecca, the witch who owned the cinema, refuse to speak to anyone apart from the sparkly bat statue outside the door? And what was the silver liquid

everyone drank every morning? And that was before she got started on her mum's weird inventions. She got the impression her mum was both admired and feared in the town – a genius who could potentially fix their every problem, but might also accidentally maim them all.

'No, no, that glove is one of my inventions, Tiga!' her mother said, twirling around the gleaming black kitchen with all the momentum of someone acting in a musical. 'I got it out of the attic just for you! It's just a bewitched glove. I call him Dennis.'

'Dennis?'

'Yes, Tiga. Dennis.'

Dennis scooped up the teapot and swivelled around, pouring it efficiently into a little puddle on the floor next to Tiga.

Tiga looked from the puddle to her mum, who was rubbing her chin.

'Never quite gets the distance right …' she mumbled, as Tiga flicked her finger and the liquid leapt obediently back into the teapot.

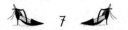 7

'You're getting very good at spells,' Gretal Green beamed.

A dress danced into the room, making Tiga jump.

'WHAT IS THAT?!'

'Another invention,' Gretal Green said proudly.

'Let me guess, it's called … Gertrude?'

'No, he's also Dennis.'

'WHAT?' Tiga cried.

'Well, I made an entire outfit, and all the parts are called Dennis.'

There was stomping coming from the attic.

'Dennis the shoes were out of control, so I locked them in the attic. Dennis the tights ran away …'

Dennis the dress floated through the air, a frilly monstrosity of lace and ribbons. It wrapped around Tiga. 'That's a hug,' Gretal Green explained.

Tiga watched as her pet slug, Sluggfrey, slimed his way across the table. He was joined by a couple of his fellow slugs, Ailbhe and Clara. When Tiga found her mum, she also discovered one of her mum's experiments – a bunch of slugs that were sent above the pipes to spy on

non-witches. They all lived in the doll's house in the hallway. All ten of them.

Who else had breakfast with pet slugs and various items of frilly bewitched clothing called Dennis?

'We're not normal witches, are we?' Tiga said.

Gretal Green cackled. 'Who wants to be a *normal* witch?'

'Me,' Tiga said quietly to herself.

'GOOD MORNING, FANS *SLASH* FAMILY!' Fran the fabulous fairy squealed as she glided into the room, shooting glittery dust everywhere. 'Isn't this wonderful! I'm visiting! And just in time for a family breakfast.'

Tiga smiled and waved at Fran as Dennis the dress turned and headed for the door. Dennis the glove leapt off the table and grabbed hold of Dennis the dress, and the pair of them disappeared into the hallway.

'Rude,' Fran said with a snort. 'That is not how you treat THE *MOST FABULOUS* FAIRY SINKVILLE HAS EVER SEEN.'

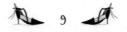

'Certainly not,' Gretal Green said with a smile. 'It's lovely to see you, Fran! Look at all the wonderful glittery dust you've brought with you!'

Fran bowed as Tiga ducked under the table and scraped some glittery dust off her tongue.

'Everyone loves glittery dust,' Fran said. 'And everyone loves me.'

'Glittery dust ...' Gretal Green said quietly as Tiga resurfaced from under the table, coughing. 'That gives me an idea ...'

'An idea?' Tiga said nervously.

'What's for breakfast, servant – I mean, Gretal Green?' Fran said, clicking her fingers.

'Oh,' Gretal Green said, completely lost in thought. Her eyebrows knitted like they always did when she was mulling over a new invention. Tiga tensed at the thought of what her mum would come up with next. 'What would you like, Fran?'

'Jam,' Fran demanded.

'Absolutely,' Gretal Green said, waving her hand. 'We haven't had jam since we returned, have we, Tiga?'

10

Tiga shook her head meekly, wondering why her mum was waving her hands.

Fran wasn't paying attention. 'Shall we sing my song "Fran, Fran, For Ever"?'

'No,' Tiga and Gretal Green said quickly as a pot of jam with long ostrich-like legs came stalking into the room.

'Another invention?' Tiga asked.

Gretal Green shook her head. 'No, the legs came free with the jam.'

Fran looked unimpressed as the jam jar leapt on to the table and smashed. Tiga looked down at the disgusting mouldy black goo.

'Ah, yes,' Gretal Green said quietly. 'I forgot I've been trapped in a hat for years. I'll need to buy some new jam.'

Fran began licking the table. 'What?' she asked, spotting Tiga's scrunched-up face. 'Aged jam is a delicacy. Probably.'

Dennis the dress came floating back into the room, a frilly arm outstretched in the direction of the jam.

'No, I will not share my fine aged jam with a … dress thing,' Fran scoffed, flopping her entire body on the table and spreading out in a starfish shape, completely covering the jam. 'Especially not a *frumpy* one.'

Dennis the dress floated on the spot.

'Shoo,' Fran said, slapping the frilly sleeve.

Tiga watched as Fran lapped up the jam. It reminded her of the weird goo Peggy'd had on her hair when she first met her. *I'm Peggy Pigwiggle. I like your mad clothes – you must be from above the pipes* echoed her friend's chirpy voice from the box in her brain filled with memories.

'Tiga?' Gretal Green asked. 'Are you all right?'

'YOU CAN'T HAVE MY JAM,' Fran said, aggressively gobbling it.

'I'm fine,' Tiga mumbled, though she wasn't really. She missed Peggy and Fluffanora and Mavis with her stall of fresh jam. She hadn't seen them in weeks; she'd been too busy settling into Silver City, getting to know her mum. She had everything she'd ever dreamed of in Silver City, apart from one thing: she didn't have her friends. She wondered what Peggy and Fluffanora were up to at that very second. *Probably having a breakfast of fresh Mavis jam, curled up on the floor of Linden House together, laughing about something*, she thought.

'TOO MUCH!' Fran roared, rolling off the table. 'I'M GOING TO BURST.'

SH TIGHTS
ANTED
ONNECTION WITH
BERY AT SILVERS,
THE GEM SHOP,
APPARENTLY

Olivia Opal, owner of Silvers, insists the robbery committed this morning at her gem shop was the work of 'a lavish pair of tights'.

Made with fine silk gauze and patterned with delicate lace, the tights trotted in and started robbing, using one leg like an arm to scoop the gems from the counter, and the other as a sort of sack.

We spoke to Olivia Opal, who said she had reported the incident to Top Witch Peggy Pigwiggle in Ritzy City.

Witches are urged to come forward if these tights sound familiar, and to check their drawers in case any of their tights may have sneaked out.

De-Cheesing

'Why do we have to de-cheese the shop *every morning*? We've been doing it *for weeks*,' Fluffanora said, plonking herself down next to the hundreds of Brew's witches who were flicking their fingers all over the shop. 'LET'S JUST ALL ADMIT THAT IT WILL ALWAYS SMELL OF CHEESE.'

'Strong spell, strong smell, we'll get it eventually,' Mrs Brew said patiently. 'Thank you for helping, too, Peggy.'

'Pleasure,' Peggy said, gagging.

'I can't believe that evil witch Miss Heks turned the shop into cheese during the good versus evil battle,' Fluffanora said, sniffing a pair of shoes. 'So unnecessary.'

Mrs Brew placed a feathery hat on a witch

mannequin. 'Well, it is a new era now. No more strange goings-on in Ritzy City. Nothing but normal life again, finally.'

'Excuse me, Mrs Brew, I found this outside,' one of her assistants said, handing her the *Silver Times* newspaper. 'I think we'd better check the tights, especially the lace ones.'

'Lavish tights … have robbed a gem shop,' Mrs Brew said.

Fluffanora cackled. 'Normal …'

Peggy straightened her shabby hat. 'We're working on that case. Oh, and I'd better go in a minute, I'm working on the old Sinkville Express railway, reconnecting the cities again! And it'll mean Tiga can visit easily.'

'Good,' Mrs Brew said. 'I don't like the thought of her trying to levitate all the way here, or riding her mum's rickety hoover.' She turned to Fluffanora. 'Could you scrape the cheese off the gloves over there, please.'

Fluffanora pretended not to hear her.

'Fluffanora!'

'Oh, all right,' she said, reluctantly. She held one up

and stared at it, wrinkling her nose in disgust. 'I miss Tiga. I bet she's having an absolutely sparkly time in Silver City …'

An extract from **The Karens,**
a very ~~terrifying~~ special book

The strange thing about the Karens was NOT that there was a whole coven of them and they were all called Karen, OR that their cat was also called Karen, although that was admittedly weird. And let's not get started on their toes. No, the strange thing about the Karens was that they cared about only one thing. And that one thing was wishes.

Have you got a wish? Because if you do, the Karens might just come knocking …

3

Lucy Tatty

Knock knock.

'I'll get it!' Tiga cried, clattering down the stairs. Gretal Green had bewitched them so they moved like escalators above the pipes, only more clunkily, and – inconveniently – upwards, so they were only really useful if you were going upstairs. Going downstairs was near impossible. Tiga gave up halfway and just levitated to the bottom, losing her balance and rolling into the door.

She reached up for the handle and flung the door open excitedly, hoping Peggy or Fluffanora had come to see her.

A pair of tights limped in.

'Oh, you're back, are you?' Gretal Green scoffed as

she came trotting down the hallway. 'Tiga, this is Dennis, the runaway tights.'

Tiga watched as the tights hopped up the stairs, one leg agile, the other filled with what looked like rocks … or jewels. They crunched and clinked on the stairs.

A witch standing at the door with a sparkling silver sack coughed impatiently and handed Tiga a newspaper.

'Oh,' Tiga said, trying not to sound too disappointed it wasn't Peggy and Fluffanora but rather a pair of tights and the post witch.

'The *Silver Times*, for Tiga and Gretal Green.'

Tiga smiled politely as Gretal Green took it and read the front page.

LAVISH TIGHTS WANTED IN CONNECTION WITH ROBBERY AT SILVERS, THE GEM SHOP, APPARENTLY

'DEEEEEENNNNNNNNNNIIISSSSSSS!'

'And a package,' the witch said, handing this one straight to Gretal Green.

'What is it?' Tiga asked, trying to read the label.

Gretal Green dropped the *Silver Times* and grabbed the package with both hands. 'The tube! The essential component for my latest, and possibly greatest, invention!' She raced up the stairs.

The witch with the sparkly sack nodded and headed off down the road, disappearing into the bustle of the Silver City morning. Tiga watched as witches swanned past, almost none of them in hats. They were probably too scared of being sucked into them and trapped, like before, she thought. The smell of salty, silvery water below wafted up and danced around Tiga as she stepped outside. The sound of waves lapping against the stilts that held the city afloat was as loud as the cackles coming from the witches clustered outside the Silver Screen Cinema next door.

'I've *never* seen a film worse than *Toe Pinchers*,' Tiga heard one say, and they erupted into cackles once more.

The platform connecting Tiga's street to the next wobbled as she walked, lost in thought. She wondered

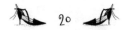

if she should ask her mum to take her to Ritzy City on her hoover, or let her borrow it and go herself. But what if her mum thought she didn't want to be with her in Silver City? Tiga didn't want to upset her. The poor witch had been stuck in a hat for years! And anyway, Peggy had *promised* she would get the Sinkville Express up and running so they could visit each other easily, but so far, no news. Peggy had probably turned the railway track into jam, Tiga imagined. Or maybe Lizzie Beast had sat on it, or something.

A whistling sound interrupted her thoughts – it was quiet at first, then ear-splittingly loud.

'INCOMING!' a witch roared.

Something that looked a lot like a basket hurtled past Tiga's head towards a little witch in front of her.

'WATCH OUT!' Tiga cried, as it landed with a thud on the girl's shoulder, knocking her to the ground with a sickening crunch.

'Frogcrutches!' she cried.

Tiga raced over. 'Are you all right?' She recognised the writing on the basket's tag. It said:

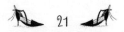

21

This is a SORRY-WE-THOUGHT-YOU-WERE-EVIL-AND-LEFT-DURING-THE-BIG-EXIT-WHEN-REALLY-YOU-WERE-JUST-SUCKED-INTO-A-HAT gift basket.

It was from Cakes, Pies and That's About It Really. Her favourite Ritzy City baker.

The young witch rubbed her head. 'They keep sending sorry baskets because they feel bad that we were trapped in hats when they thought we were evil and left Sinkville during the Big Exit.'

Tiga looked up and saw hundreds of the baskets raining down on the city, knocking witches over, crashing through roofs and windows.

'I really love your outfit!' the girl squeaked, leaping to her feet.

Tiga smoothed her metallic silver skirt. She'd teamed it with a lace top and some stripy braces. She looked at what the young witch was wearing. 'I like your outfit, too –' She stopped. The young witch was wearing something very familiar.

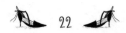

'Is that …?' Tiga shook her head and looked again.

Perhaps she was seeing things.

No, she was right.

'That's my Witch Wars outfit, isn't it?'

At that, the girl practically choked. She started urgently rummaging around in her backpack and pulled out a piece of paper titled WITCH WARS FAN PACK (Warning: Contains Cats).

A cat leapt from the backpack and scurried off down the road.

'IT'S YOU!' the girl roared, pointing a finger at the picture of Tiga and then squidging her finger on Tiga's nose. 'YOU'RE TIGA WHICABIM NOW GREEN!'

Tiga suddenly felt incredibly self-conscious. This was definitely more something Fran would appreciate. 'Um … yes, I suppose I am.'

The girl's eyes widened and she rummaged in her backpack some more, reaching in so far, Tiga was sure she was going to disappear into it completely.

'I'm Lucy. Lucy Tatty. I made the outfit myself. And I am your *number one* fan!'

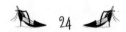

Tiga noticed the backpack was covered in scribbly sketches of her face, and Fran's, and Peggy's, even Felicity Bat's.

'I just finished watching *Witch Wars* the other day. I was late to watch it because I was stuck in a hat, but now I've seen every episode and all the reruns. They show it all the time on Fairy 5.' She pulled a map out of her bag. There was a gigantic sparkly cross over Tiga's house. 'I was actually coming to see where you lived. It took me days to figure it out, but this is where I think it is. Is it?' She thrust the map in Tiga's face.

'Uh, yes,' Tiga said, as another basket came crashing down and sent a cat flying.

'Poor thing!' Lucy cried. 'When I'm older I'm going to open a centre for cats having a bad day. I'll call it The Centre for Cats Having a Bad Day. Or Happy Fluff, or something …'

'Sounds good,' Tiga said wearily as Lucy Tatty pulled a shrivelled head out of her bag.

'Will you sign my shrivelled head? I also made it.'

Tiga took it to sign it.

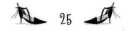

'Out of paper – and a big old ball of soggy cat hair.'

'Ugh!' Tiga squealed, dropping it on the ground.

'NEVER MIND!' Lucy Tatty said, leaping from foot to foot next to the now slightly bashed thing. 'I'll make a new one later, I have lots of cats! I'm Lucy Tatty and I'm your number one fan.'

'Yes,' Tiga said. 'You mentioned that. Wait, Tatty? You know, my best friend, Fluffanora, loves a book called *Melissa's Broken Broom*. It's written by a witch called *Gloria* Tatty!'

The girl scrunched up her face. 'Fluffanora said Witch Wars was *silly*. That's why she's not on my bag. I drew a mash-up of yours and Fran's faces instead.'

'Lovely,' Tiga said, inspecting the bag. One of the doodles featured a speech bubble with I'M FABU-LOUS! And was essentially Tiga with Fran's body, hair and glasses.

'But Fluffanora was nice to you so I like her now. And yes, Gloria Tatty is my granny.'

'Cool!' Tiga said. 'Does she live in Silver City?'

'No, she lives at Rainbow Bones, in the towers. It's

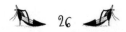

a place for exceptionally old witches. All her books are in the Silver Stacks bookshop. Do you regret letting Peggy win?'

'Uh, well, no,' Tiga said, barely able to keep up.

'Does Crispy smell?'

Tiga shook her head.

'Tiga!' Gretal Green shouted from the window. 'What are you doing over there?'

'I'm going to show her the best bookshop in Silver City!' Lucy Tatty called up. 'They've just released a new book about Witch Wars called *Witch Wars: The Bloopers*, see.' She pulled a flyer from her bag. The cover showed Tiga fast asleep with her mouth wide open, and Fran shining her shoes on Tiga's tongue.

'That didn't happen!' Tiga cried. 'Did it?'

'A bookshop! What a lovely idea!' Gretal Green said, before being distracted by a pair of tights bouncing off down the road. 'DEEEEENNNNIIIISSSS! COME BACK HERE RIGHT NOW!'

'Do you think Aggie Hoof wishes she was Fluffanora? Do you think Felicity Bat is an idiot? Do you think

Peggy is the best witch in the world? Is Fran's hair real?' Lucy Tatty plonked her backpack on the ground and started pulling things out of it. 'I have a Fran-style wig in here somewhere ... I made it out of cat hair ...'

'Come on,' Tiga said, hoisting little Lucy to her feet. 'Let's go see this brilliant bookshop you were talking about.'

'Oh goody!' Lucy said, twirling around and latching on to Tiga's arm. 'I'm Lucy Tatty, and I'm your number one fan.'

'Yes,' Tiga said faintly. 'You said ...'

Another extract from The Karens, *a really ~~terrifying~~ special book*

The Karens are a bit like genies, only much better. And they don't live in a RIDICULOUS lamp! They live in a jelly castle.

The castle is a gigantic, sprawling feast for the eyes, with many turrets added to the place over

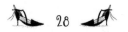

28

the years. There are thirteen Karens in total, including one Senior Karen, who is in charge of all the others.

The Karens guarantee one hundred per cent wish satisfaction. Only a couple of witches have dared return to the castle, unhappy with the results of their wishes. But they all failed to get to them, because their jelly castle has excellent defences against idiots.

Let's see, there was Lydia Pond – who, fittingly, failed because she fell in a pond. The Karens found that very funny indeed.

Then there was Simona Fence, who could not get over the fence the Karens had built around their jelly castle.

And we must not forget Susanna Goteaten, who took one look at the Karens and ran away.

The Karens pride themselves on being the best wish-granters in the land, better than any genie you've ever met: that, they guarantee. So come along and make a wish! Show your friends this book!

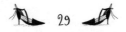

Silver Stacks

The Silver Stacks bookshop looked quite different to when Tiga had first seen it.

When she'd visited the place looking for her mum, it was nothing but dust, cobwebs and very well read spiders. Now the silver exterior glistened in the light, and inside, neon-coloured books floated through the air, tapping witches on the shoulder every now and again.

'The books can fly?'

Lucy Tatty laughed. 'The books are for sale, so they're doing their selling thing, aren't they?'

Tiga watched as a copy of *Melissa's Broken Broom* bobbed through the air and aggressively bopped an old witch on the head.

'It's funny you don't know these things because you lived above the pipes for so long with that Miss Heks woman,' Lucy rambled on. 'Why did she really like cheese? Did she ever have a cheese-water *bath*? I read that somewhere. Was your shed leaky?'

'Has your gran written anything else?' Tiga asked, trying to change the subject from horrible Miss Heks.

'No, just *Melissa's Broken Broom*, we have lots over here, I'll show you.' She reached into her bag and pulled a Miss Heks puppet out of it. 'I made it so I could pretend I was you. I put a sound thing in her so she screams CHEESE WATER!'

She pulled the string at the back.

'Please …' Tiga managed to say. 'No …'

'CHEESE WATER,' the doll groaned as Lucy came lunging at her with the thing.

Tiga stumbled backwards and smacked straight into a bookcase. It wobbled slightly. 'Uh-oh …' she said, as the entire thing came crashing down on her.

Lucy stood over the mound of books and crumpled Tiga. 'Oops.'

Slowly Tiga got to her feet, clutching the wall's faded grey bricks.

Lucy Tatty skipped on the spot. 'Are Fran's glasses real or just for decoration?'

Tiga stopped. Something caught her eye, wedged in the wall, glowing. She reached past and stretched her fingers. She could feel it! She wiggled the bricks until one began to come loose.

'What are you doing, Tiga my favourite Witch Wars contestant *ever*?'

Tiga wasn't listening to Lucy Tatty. It was almost like she was underwater – everything she could hear was just a warble of whooshing and humming.

'Got it!' Tiga shouted, making everyone jump.

Lucy Tatty glanced cautiously at the bookshelf. 'Got what? Is it a Witch Wars thing?'

Tiga pulled it out and stared at it. It wasn't glowing at all, but it definitely had been, hadn't it? She shook it. Dust fell in large clumps to the ground.

'It was shiny a minute ago …' she said slowly.

'What was?' Lucy Tatty asked.

Tiga wiped the cover with her sleeve.

'This book,' she said, holding it up so Lucy Tatty could see. '*The Karens*, by Gloria Tatty.'

5

Tube Fairy

'What's that you've got there, Tiga?' Fran asked, swooping in and flicking the book open. Her eyes widened as she read the first page. 'These Karens are really weird … but I love the Jelly Castle.' She spotted Lucy. 'She's dressed like you and has crazy eyes,' she mumbled to Tiga out of the side of her mouth. 'Walk away slowly …'

'No, Fran, this is Lucy Tatty and she is a huge fan of Witch Wars.'

'WELL WHY DIDN'T YOU SAY?' Fran bellowed, shooting glittery dust in Lucy's face.

Lucy bent over double and began heaving.

'It's wonderful to meet one of my biggest fans, Lucy. You can keep that glittery dust if you want. Bottle it up, keep it on a shelf, prominently displayed, and you can boast, "I got that from Fran, the most fabulous fairy in all of Sinkville." If you want.'

'I've done it! I've only gone and done it!' came a voice from outside the bookshop.

Tiga spotted her mother cantering past, holding a tiny tube above her head.

'Is something fabulous happening without me?' Fran asked.

Tiga snapped the book shut as Fran glided eagerly towards the door. A squat little witch carrying books stacked up to her armpits raced to the door, too.

'Oh, Lady Stacks!' Lucy shouted after her. 'This is Tiga, my new friend from Witch Wars!' But she wasn't listening.

'She created a new fairy!' a witch outside shouted. 'It's a miracle!'

Lucy Tatty rolled her eyes. 'That's not a miracle. A miracle is a spell you do and then don't tell anyone you've done it.'

Whatever it was, Tiga couldn't quite believe what she was hearing. Her mum, *her* mum, had created an

actual fairy. Fran was going to kill her.

'THIS,' Gretal Green shouted from the fountain she was precariously perched on, 'is a brand new fairy. Fairies are wonderful things.'

'Hear hear!' Fran shouted. Tiga looked up, surprised. Clearly Fran hadn't caught the bit about the *new fairy*.

'This is all about me, isn't it,' Fran said, rubbing her hands together.

'Fairies,' Gretal Green went on, 'look after us.'

'Well …' Fran said. 'Not really a priority, but –'

'And fairies produce a remarkable substance – glittery dust! We are the sparkliest city in all of Sinkville so we should have an abundance of glittery dust!'

There was a ripple of whispers throughout the crowd. Tiga groaned. Glittery dust was the worst.

'Imagine what we could do with extra fairies! We could make the place look even more wonderful. And just think – if fairies had been around in Silver City when we were all sucked into our hats, they would've said something to the witches in Ritzy City and we wouldn't have been stuck for so long!'

The whispers from the crowd turned into excitable squeaks.

'This doesn't feel like it's massively about me any more …' Fran said, an eyebrow raised.

'Fairies keep us safe, and make things sparkly. Fran the Fabulous Fairy is the reason I came up with this! She is a wonderful fairy who has looked after my daughter.'

'Don't forget how famous that fairy is!' Fran shouted from the crowd.

'Oh, here she is now!' Gretal Green said.

Fran flew eagerly through the crowd, soaking up the claps and admiration as she went. 'No really, stop it! Stop it!'

Gretal Green hushed the crowd and held up a tiny test tube. 'I wanted to see if we could use some of Fran's glittery dust to make new fairies.'

Tiga watched as Fran felt around in her skirt. That was where she kept her glittery dust. She looked a bit miffed.

'I only took a smidge of the stuff you left in the kitchen this morning,' Gretal Green insisted. 'Did a bit of fiddling with this little tube and some toenails and whatnot.'

The crowd groaned.

'And I created *this*!'

She took the stopper off the test tube and a burst of colourful dust shot into the air, making everyone gasp.

'It only took me four minutes,' she added, proudly.

There was a silence as the glowing little thing floated down.

Tiga winced. 'Uh-oh.'

Lucy looked at her. 'Why uh-oh? She's perfect!'

'Exactly,' said Tiga. 'Just wait.'

'YOU CREATED THIS MONSTROSITY?! PUT IT BACK IN ITS LITTLE TUBE!' Fran bellowed.

A gorgeous fairy hovered gracefully, waving and winking at the crowd. She had glossy blonde hair, bright white teeth and sparkly eyes. A prototype fairy. The kind Tiga had read about in books above the pipes. The fairy giggled.

'I'M BORED OF IT ALREADY, PUT IT AWAY!' Fran tried again, but the crowd was mesmerised.

'She's perfect!'

'She's wonderful!'

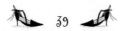

39

'I want one!'

'I want to *be* one!'

Tiga covered her eyes. She couldn't watch.

'I mean, she's all right …' Fran grumbled, inspecting the little fairy's hair and tugging on it slightly, clearly hoping it was a wig. 'But as the best fairy of *all time*, I still vote that we put her back in the little tube thingy.'

6

A Fabulous Complaint

The next day, Felicity Bat levitated into the Linden House sitting room, where Top Witch Peggy Pigwiggle was pacing. She had a number of pressing things to deal with – getting the Sinkville Express up and running, opening a new school in the Docks, and Mavis, who was petitioning to change the shape of all jam jars so they were the same shape as cats.

'Pegs, did you see the papers this morning?'

She'd hired the once-evil-but-now-just-a-bit-grumpy Felicity Bat to be her adviser. They made a strange pair – one slick and sour faced, the other a bouncing ball of curly hair and hope.

Peggy shook her head as Felicity Bat threw the newspaper across the room.

GRETAL GREEN
INVENTS
AN ENTIRE FAIRY!

The ingenious inventor and NAPA employee Gretal Green has created Sinkville's first test tube fairy in a bid to increase fairy numbers again. The idea was inspired by Fran, who accompanied Green and her daughter, Tiga, to Silver City to help Tiga settle in. Tiga had been living with the famous Brew family in Ritzy City after not winning Witch Wars and before finding her mother.

The fairy has decided to call herself Zarkle and wishes, in her exact words, 'to spread joy, smiles and perfection and be the best fairy Sinkville has ever seen!' We visited the Fairy Caravan Park to ask Crispy the fairy what she made of the news, but Crispy couldn't stop laughing, between wheezes of 'Fran' and 'War'.

'Does Fran *know* yet?' Peggy spluttered.

Felicity Bat smiled. 'That was the next thing I was going to talk to you about …' She opened the door and in shot a blur of beehive and glitter.

'Your Top Witchiness, it is I, FRAN! I am here to file a very serious complaint about a sort-of fairy!'

Peggy listened patiently, trying not to laugh as Fran re-enacted the reveal of Gretal Green's new fairy.

'So we should squash her or put her in a glass jar or –' She stopped when she spotted Peggy's horrified face. 'Or … something less brutal but equally effective?'

Peggy patted the fairy's beehive gently. 'Fran –'

'Watch the hair!' Fran said, recoiling.

'Fran,' Peggy tried again. 'I really don't think I can – or would want to – squash another fairy. And trapping her in a jar would be cruel.'

'Would it?' Fran asked, giving Peggy a playful nudge.

'Yes,' Felicity Bat said.

'And if Felicity Bat of all witches thinks it's cruel,' Peggy whispered to Fran, giving her a wink, but Fran crossed her arms and stared off in the other direction.

'If Tiga was in charge of Sinkville, she would squash the new fairy for me.'

'Fran,' Peggy said. 'I have bigger problems to deal with. Mavis wants to change the shape of jam jars so they are the exact same shape as a cat.'

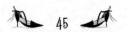
45

Fran thought about that for a moment.

'Cat-shaped jam jars, Fran.'

'I'm sorry,' Fran said slowly. 'It sounds like you just said cat-shaped jam jars are more important than A FAIRY IN DISTRESS?'

Peggy tried to place a finger on Fran's shoulder, but Fran just shook her off, fluffed her beehive of hair dramatically and headed towards the door. 'Well, I have to do my *Cooking for Tiny People* show now. I shall have to fix this new fairy stuff myself, and I shall fix it *fabulously*.'

Fluffenwaffle

'You're taller in real life,' Lucy Tatty said, clinging to Tiga's arm as they strolled along Silver City's winding walkways the following day. It was becoming clear to Tiga that Lucy Tatty wasn't going anywhere.

'So you didn't know your gran wrote *The Karens*?' Tiga asked. Witches trotted past them, occasionally being knocked to the ground by one of the many wayward Cakes, Pies and That's About It Really gift baskets that were still hurtling through the air.

Lucy Tatty ducked to avoid one while holding the book at arm's length like it was an aggressive cat. 'No, I've definitely never seen this book before!'

'Well, it doesn't look finished. Maybe she never got around to finishing it! What a discovery!'

'I could BURST with excitement.' Lucy Tatty beamed. 'You should show your friend Flufflewaffle who likes my gran's other book!'

'It's Fluff*anora* ...'

'That's what I said, isn't it?' Lucy Tatty said. 'Fluffentruffle, the one who thought Witch Wars was silly. Oh no, wait, Fluff*anora*. How many times do you think you've cuddled Peggy? Tiga? Tiga?' She trotted after Tiga, the book hanging at her side. She was so focused on catching up with Tiga that she completely missed the little letter that slipped from the book and fell into the choppy water below.

8

Cooking for Tiny People

'WHAAAAAAAT?!' Fran roared as she flew on to set.

'Isn't she fabulous?' Patricia the producer oozed. 'She's called *Zarkle*. It's Gretal Green's new fairy invention.'

'If that's your kind of thing,' Fran said, trying her best to remain composed. Tiny lumps of glitter were puffing from her collar. Zarkle and her silly name had somehow made her way on to the set. 'Patricia,' Fran said urgently. 'I wanted to run my recipe for today's episode past you. My best yet! It's called FINE AGED JAM, and we'll sit and stare at some fine aged jam – looking *fabulous*, of course – and then we'll say, 'And after you wait around eight years, *this* is what you'll get.' And I'll show some fine aged jam. I know where to get it. My fan-family, the

Greens in Silver City, have many jars.'

Patricia the producer tapped Fran hastily on the beehive. 'Actually, I've asked Zarkle to present today. Mix things up a bit.'

Fran blinked at her.

'Zarkle, Fran. She's going to do a recipe today.'

Fran blinked at her.

'ZARKLE, FRAN!'

Fran nodded and then, in her best booming voice, managed to squeak, 'WELL ALL RIGHTY THEN! I'LL JUST GET OUT OF YOUR HAIR, AND *HER* PERFECT HAIR.'

They all watched as she flew calmly out of the door.

'Well, that went well,' Patricia the producer said to Crispy, as Zarkle twirled next to the fridge.

Crispy put on a helmet.

Patricia the producer raised an eyebrow. 'Why the helmet, Crispy?'

'War,' Crispy said with a knowing nod. 'This will mean war.'

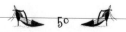

9
Smash!

Fran clattered about in her caravan, a spoon propped up on the chaise longue in the corner.

The spoon was showing the live Fairy Network coverage of Zarkle on *Cooking for Tiny People*.

The camera kept dropping slightly, like Crispy was letting go of it or falling asleep.

'I went with the name Zarkle because it means the highest grade of sparkle and I am the highest grade of fairy,' she said with a giggle.

'Pah!' Fran spat, before turning and frantically thumbing through a tiny dictionary.

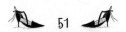

FAIRY WORDS

Zarkle
\Zark-al
To sparkle brighter than anything and ANYONE else.

Examples
I wish I could zarkle like that.
There's sparkle, and then there's zarkle.

Origin
Old Witchlish, seventh century. Used by the founding witches of Sinkville, most commonly when complaining about bright spells, for example: THAT SPELL IS ZARKLING MY EYE-BALLS, ANNABELLE.

'It was originally an offensive word!' Fran said, pleased with herself. 'Used to yell at a witch called Annabelle.' But there was no one in her caravan to hear her.

She grunted as she pulled at a sparkly rope leading all the way out of the door of her caravan. She dropped the spoon and held the rope tightly with both hands.

'FABULOUS HEAVE!' she shouted. 'FABULOUS HEAVE!'

Outside, a jam jar with TRAP scrawled on it in sparkly paint dangled on the end of the rope.

'This is the perfect trap,' Fran said, in her best villain voice. 'The perfect trap jar.'

She was lost in thoughts of trapping Zarkle and hiding her in the *Cooking for Tiny People* fridge when a letter – a large one, smartly typed – squeezed its way through the door.

'Huh?' Fran mumbled, slipping slightly and letting go of the rope. There was an almighty crunch outside. She peeked out of the door.

'FROGTRUFFLENUTWAFFLES! My Zarkle trap!' she squealed, looking down at the shattered pieces.

And that's when she saw what was written on the letter.

DO YOU WISH YOU WERE BIGGER SO YOU COULD EASILY HOLD A JAM JAR WITH 'TRAP' WRITTEN ON IT?

You saw our book - you know that WE CAN MAKE YOUR WISHES COME TRUE (not like a genie, we're better than that rubbish).

VISIT THE KARENS! Fly to us at:
  The Jelly Castle,
  Boulder Boulevard,
  The Badlands,
  Sinkville.

Strictly no hot Clutterbucks cocktails please.

Helmet

'Aaaany second now,' Crispy said, tapping her helmet. 'Fran will be back aaaany second now.'

Patricia the producer tapped her foot impatiently. 'Stop tapping your helmet, Crispy,' she snapped. 'Every time you do it, you wobble the camera and we are *live*. Fran isn't coming back. And can you please stop muttering things about war!'

Crispy stared at the door with her tiny squashed eyes. 'She'll be back,' she said quietly, more to herself than anyone else. 'I know Fran.'

'Oh, for the love of a frog playing hopscotch, GET OUT, CRISPY! I'll do the filming myself.'

Crispy jumped off her little director-style chair and walked, head down, towards the door. She turned back.

'Really, Patricia the producer?'

Patricia the producer bent down so she was nose to nose with Crispy. 'REALLY.'

And so out Crispy walked, as Zarkle inspected her teeth in the reflection on the fridge.

'I LOVE TEETH I DO,' the perfect fairy said, in a surprisingly gruff voice.

HOLIDAY FOR BROOMS

Wonderful news: Peggy Pigwiggle has reinstated the Sinkville Express train, allowing witches high-speed travel to their favourite Sinkville destinations! The train will travel its original route – as far as Pearl Peak, stopping at the Towers, Brollywood, the Docks, Ritzy City, Driptown, all the way to Silver City before looping around the Badlands and back to Silver City.

The Ritzy City station will have stalls and a Clutterbucks dispenser and Mavis's new diffusion line of jam, which will be sold in jam jars shaped like cats, despite everyone's efforts to stop her being so ridiculous.

The railway was originally built by Lucinda Bunch, an engineer known for her obsessive note-taking and favourite saying: 'Everything can always go faster.' It was closed down during evil Celia Crayfish's reign, as she wanted to cut off easy contact between the cities, carving up Sinkville like pieces of tart.

But we are united once more! The railway will officially open in the morning, according to Peggy Pigwiggle and assisting Top Witch Felicity Bat. It is a must-do in Sinkville. Jump aboard now! It's free – zero sinkels!

IMPORTANT PUBLIC NOTICE FROM BRELLA RELLA'S UMBRELLA SHOP: You know when you wave an umbrella about and someone always shouts, 'Be careful! You'll poke someone's eye out!' Turns out this is especially true if your umbrella is made of steel. Apologies to Isabel Tutt.

ADVERTISEMENT

WANTED: an effective recipe for an eyeball repair spell, or just an eyeball. Please contact Isabel Tutt at 47 Swivel Heights, Silver City, Sinkville.

11

The Clutterbucks Pipe and Peggy's Letter

Tiga lay on her bed reading *The Karens*. It wasn't much of a story – just some boastful pages about a coven of witches called Karen and how wonderful they were compared to genies. She watched Sluggfrey flop over on the bed and fall asleep, and wondered if maybe Gloria Tatty had fallen asleep when writing it.

'Evening post!' her mum said, popping her head around the door and sending a letter sailing over to Tiga. It was stamped with the unmistakable purple T.W. of the Top Witch.

'Peggy!' Tiga cried as she tore it open, flinging the envelope to the bottom of the bed. Sluggfrey opened one eye, spotted it and slimed over, curling up in it as if it was a sleeping bag. A pipe next to Tiga's bed spat some

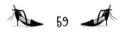

glistening liquid into a cup. Her mum had created a Clutterbucks pipe for her – it was magically linked to the café all the way back in Ritzy City so she could have Clutterbucks drinks any time she wanted. It wasn't quite the same as drinking them with Peggy and Fluffanora, though.

She took a sip and read the letter.

Dear Tiga,

I'm sorry it's taken me ages to write to you! Everything has been so hectic, and also Felicity Bat ate all the blank paper in Linden House (I think it's some sort of side effect of turning good …).

Aggie Hoof has been hanging around Linden House a lot. A lot. She keeps trying to dress me and I keep finding it impossible to say no. I'm writing this to you wearing so many bracelets on my arms I can't even bend them.

The good news is I've managed to get the Sinkville Express up and running. It took a long time because Celia Crayfish had really messed with it. The first journey is tomorrow and I've saved you a space! Go to

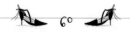

Silver City station tomorrow and they'll take you to your special Sinkville Express carriage. Also, could you bring Fran? She came to Linden House to ask if I would kill that new fairy your mum invented and I said no – and now I can't get hold of her. She doesn't seem to be in any of her favourite spots – the Fairy Caravan Park, the Cooking for Tiny People *set, shouting at Julie Jumbo Wings. So I hope she's with you?*

I can't wait to see you – everyone misses you so much (especially ME).

Love from Peggy

'Fran isn't with me …' Tiga mumbled in Sluggfrey's direction. 'And she isn't there. I wonder where she – ?'

'Whatcha reading?' came a voice from the window, making Tiga scream.

Lucy heaved herself through and flopped down on the bed, nearly squashing Sluggfrey.

'I just have some more questions, as your number one fan. What is your favourite colour? Do you like Peggy or Fran more? Is Peggy as nice as she seems on

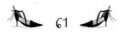

TV? Does Aggie Hoof's scream really sound like that or did they use special effects? What's that letter about? Is it from Peggy?'

Tiga shoved the letter under her pillow. 'It's nothing,' she said. 'You'd better go home – it's getting late.'

'Oh, that's no problem at all,' Lucy said with a smile. 'I put a hat by my pillow and a load of cats in my bed so my mum will think it's me.'

'Won't the cats just climb out of the bed?'

'FROGNUGGETS!' Lucy cried as she clattered out of the door.

12

All Aboard!

'ALL ABOARD THE SINKVILLE EXPRESS!' a witch chimed. Her skirt had a train print on it, and she was wearing a hat with an actual mini train zooming around the brim.

'QUICKLY, I DON'T HAVE ALL DAY!'

Tiga stepped up into one of the carriages. It was a beautifully ornate train – all open sides and plump black cushions.

'TIGA!' came a familiar voice. 'WAIT FOR ME!'

Tiga looked around and saw Lucy Tatty scurrying towards her, her huge backpack weighing her down. 'I'm Tiga's number one fan, excuse me, coming through. Make way for Tiga's number one fan, thank you.'

She wedged herself between Tiga and the edge of the

carriage, even though there was an entirely empty seat on the other side.

'How did you know – ?' Tiga began.

'I saw that the letter was from Peggy – that purple T.W. – and I heard the Sinkville Express was opening up again, so I put two and two together.' She leaned in and said seriously, in a hushed voice, 'I think I could beat Felicity Bat with all this brain power.' She tapped her head.

Tiga forced a smile.

'I can't wait to meet everyone,' Lucy said, as she pulled an old shoe out from under one of the pillows.

An incredibly old and frail witch leaned into the carriage and snatched it. '*Mine.* Left it here eighty years ago.' Tiga noticed she was only wearing one shoe and her other foot was clad in nothing more than the remnants of a sock.

'Why didn't she buy another pair of shoes?' she whispered to Lucy.

The old woman slipped on the other shoe and took off like a rocket. 'WHEEEEEEE!'

'That's why,' Lucy Tatty said, as the old lady disappeared with a little *ting* in the distance. 'Those are Shoes by Karen, Who Really Struggles to Think of Cool Shop Names. It's Silver City's best shoe shop. Karen's shoes back in the day were like rockets. My gran said it was weird because her name wasn't even Karen, it was Eddie. They don't make them like that any more.'

'Shame,' Tiga said, grabbing on to her seat as the train began to rattle.

And off they shot.

☆⭐☆

They tore through the cold air high above the glistening silver stilts of the city, and soon they were hurtling towards Ritzy. Lucy grinned and pointed at the book Tiga was clutching tightly.

'Fluffentruffle's going to love my gran's book!'

Tiga turned to see the city's glistening mismatched roofs poking through the clouds.

'SPEED REDUCING! NEXT STOP RITZY CITY CENTRAL!'

'It'll be great to see it with someone who really knows the place,' Lucy Tatty said, leaning over the edge to have a good look. 'I've only ever visited once, when I was really little. Oh, also –' She reached into her backpack and pulled out a necklace of homemade shrivelled heads. 'I made this last night. I'm going to get everyone to sign their face! I even made a Fluffanora, and I drew her on my bag.' She turned the backpack towards Tiga and pointed at a scrunched scribble right by the bottom seam.

'I'm sure she'll be delighted …' Tiga said, leaning over the edge of the carriage. 'Look! That's Brew's. And there's Mavis, the jam stall owner! MAVIS!'

She laughed as Mavis picked up one of her jars of jam, looking very confused, and whispered 'Hello?' to it.

Lucy laughed too, even though she had no idea what Tiga was laughing at.

'You know, Tiga,' Lucy said. 'I'm your number one fan.'

Tiga smiled just as another letter slipped from the book on to the seat next to her.

TIGA LETTER: Second attempt to get in touch with Tiga.

But neither Tiga nor Lucy spotted it.

Tiga sighed. 'Yes, I know you're my number one fa–'

There was an almighty screech. The train wobbled; the tracks seemed to bend.

'IS THIS MEANT TO HAPPEN?' Lucy roared. 'Or is it an unexpected thing, like when you realised Felicity Bat had been *cheating* in Witch Wars?'

Tiga clung on to the side as the entire carriage detached from the track and hurtled towards the ground. The letter was sent soaring off in the other direction and landed neatly in a bin, without Tiga noticing a thing.

The carriage plummeted towards the market stalls below.

'Fraaaaaan, heeeeeelp!' Tiga instinctively cried.

'I'M YOUR NUMBER ONE FAN!' Lucy Tatty roared in her ear.

They spiralled down and landed with a *CRUNCH* on Mavis's jam stall.

69

'Oh, I only just fixed the roof!' Mavis ranted, as Tiga looked up at her sheepishly.

'TIIIIIGA! It's you. Everyone as you were! Nothing to see here!' She stretched out a hand and pulled Tiga from the ramshackle mess of spilled jam and stall walls. 'You can break my stall anytime, you hear! Anytime.'

Tiga gave her a big hug. Lucy got to her feet and dusted herself down. One of Mavis's cats growled at her.

'This is Lucy,' Tiga said.

'YOU ARE NOT ALLOWED TO TAKE THE CARRIAGES!' the woman in the train-patterned skirt yelled down to them as the carriage floated back up and reattached itself to the track.

'TIGA! IT'S TIGA!' came a familiar cry. Peggy collided with Tiga, knocking her to the ground. 'I was going to collect you from the station. Why did you arrive … on Mavis's jam stall?'

'It's you!' Fluffanora squealed, piling on top of them. 'Tiga! You're back!'

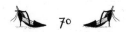

76

Mrs Brew, who was practically in tears at the sight of her, came racing over. She lifted Tiga to her feet and twirled her round and round. 'What do you think of Silver City? Are you having a wonderful ti–'

She stopped and looked from Tiga to Mavis's stall and back again. 'Did you try to levitate here and crash-land? I told you girls to encourage Tiga to get the train.'

'I *did* get the train,' Tiga explained, as Mavis nodded solemnly. 'It fell off the track.'

'Well, that's worrying,' Peggy mumbled.

Fluffanora patted her on the back. 'You just love falling on that stall roof, don't you, Tiga …'

'I'm Lucy Tatty,' the little witch said, jumping between them and staring up at Peggy like she was inspecting a rare beast. 'You look less messy in real life! I wanted Tiga to win Witch Wars. How many spells can you do now? Do you still use Flappy Flora's Floral Foot Cream?'

'She's just watched *Witch Wars*,' Tiga whispered apologetically.

'Is she wearing your Witch Wars outfit?' Fluffanora asked quietly.

Tiga nodded. 'Made it herself.'

'It's lovely to meet you, Lucy Tatty,' Peggy said sweetly, as Lucy thrust a shrunken head in her face.

'I haven't seen something like that since Witch Wars!' Peggy laughed.

'I made it out of soggy old cat hair and paper, can

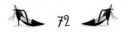

you sign it? Thank you,' Lucy said, as Fluffanora gagged behind her.

She swivelled to face Fluffanora. 'And I know almost nothing about you, because you were knocked out of Witch Wars early, but Tiga said you would like to know that my gran wrote *Melissa's Broken Broom*.'

'Wait, your *gran* is Gloria Tatty?!'

Lucy nodded and handed Fluffanora the book. 'We found this unfinished book by her. Tiga said you'd want to see it!'

Fluffanora, who Tiga normally saw in only two modes – cool and composed or stylish but grumpy – looked like she was about to melt with joy. She held the book gently in her hands and opened it.

'Cool, isn't it?' Tiga said.

Fluffanora cackled. 'Goodness, Fran must be delighted!'

'Fran?' Tiga and Lucy said at the same time.

'Yeah,' Fluffanora said, holding the book up and pointing at a page. 'She's in it.'

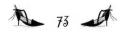

'Where is Fran?' Peggy asked, looking around expectantly.

'She wasn't with me,' Tiga said. 'You haven't seen her yet?'

'No,' Peggy said slowly. 'She hasn't been seen for days …'

'How strange,' Tiga said, running her hand over the book.

'She's probably getting her hair done,' Fluffanora said, dismissively. 'Come on, let's go to Clutterbucks.'

Tiga stared at the page Fluffanora had been reading. It looked like an illustration of Fran … only she was bigger, more witch-sized. And she was dressed like a princess. She also appeared to be in, well, a *jelly* castle.

'Is that a jelly castle?' a familiar voice said.

'Oh, hi, Felicity,' Tiga said, giving her a hug, which was sort of like hugging an aggressive plank of wood. 'This is Lucy.'

'Nice to meet you, Lucy,' Felicity Bat said with a bow.

'She used to be evil but now she's almost nice,' Peggy explained.

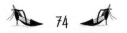

'I'M NOT GOING ANYWHERE NEAR HER,' Lucy Tatty said, holding her backpack in front of her face.

'Who brought the mini Tiga?' Felicity Bat said.

'She's a Witch Wars fan from Silver City,' Peggy said, slowly pushing down the backpack from in front of Lucy's face. 'And we are *thrilled* to have her here!'

Felicity Bat rolled her eyes. 'What's the weird book about, then? Princesses in jelly castles?'

Tiga thrust the book into Felicity Bat's hand. 'It's the weirdest thing. We found this.'

'*The Karens* by Gloria Tatty,' Felicity Bat read.

'Yes,' Tiga went on. 'But the book wasn't finished. It ended at this page.' She tapped it.

'So?' Felicity Bat said.

'But now, since we last looked, it ends on *this* page.'

Felicity Bat narrowed her eyes and inspected it closely. 'Is that Fran?'

Tiga nodded. 'Only she looks big. And she's a princess. In a jelly castle.'

'You know,' Felicity Bat said, closing the book and handing it back to her. 'Ritzy City is only ever nuts when you're here.'

Tiga's face fell.

'But also lots of fun too!' Peggy said, giving Tiga an encouraging nudge.

'You probably just didn't see the page,' Fluffanora said.

Tiga stared at the book. She was sure one of the Karens on the front cover winked at her. She shook her head. *Stop being weird, Tiga.*

'Stop being weird, Tiga,' Felicity Bat said.

'I was thinking exactly that!' Tiga cried.

'I know,' Felicity Bat said flatly. 'I'm perfecting my mind-reading spells today.'

'BUT SHE PROMISES NOT TO USE THEM FOR EVIL, D-O-E-S-N-'T SHE,' Peggy said sternly.

Felicity Bat nodded like an obedient cat.

EXCLUSIVE INTERVIEW WITH SINKVILLE EXPRESS DRIVER GAYLE GOSTEAM!

Gayle Gosteam is the driver of the Sinkville Express. She was originally hired to drive the train by Lucinda Bunch when the line first opened many, many years ago, and now Peggy Pigwiggle has rehired her.

Gayle Gosteam lost her job when evil Top Witch Celia Crayfish closed down the railway network. Afterwards, she went to the Coves and swapped train driving for partying, roller-skating and eating cake. She was the first and only train driver in Sinkville and did strenuous training above the pipes, driving lots of angry non-witches to work every day.

Now Gayle's back in the driving seat, and our reporter sat down for an exclusive interview with this fascinating witch!

Reporter: Hello, Gayle Gosteam.
Gayle Gosteam: Hello.
Reporter: Gayle, you like trains, don't you?
Gayle Gosteam: Love them.
Reporter: Me too. Do you also like planes?
Gayle Gosteam: Not as much.
Reporter: Cars?
Gayle Gosteam: Not as much as trains.
Reporter: Boats?
Gayle Gosteam: Um ... are these your questions?
Reporter: Donkeys?

13

Clutterbucks

'Whoa!' Lucy Tatty said, taking a seat at one of the floating tables. 'Who do you each like the most? Peggy? Tiga?'

'Definitely not Tiga,' Felicity Bat said, rolling her eyes.

'Wonderful to see you all!' Mrs Clutterbuck said with a chuckle. 'Tiga, we miss you around here.' She clapped her hands and a huge cake and a selection of their favourite Clutterbucks cocktails landed on the table. 'Enjoy.'

Tiga was still flicking through the book. 'I mean, we must've just missed it. But I'm *sure* this page wasn't here before.'

'Why are you so worried about the book?' Peggy asked.

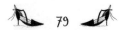

Tiga looked up at them all. 'Because. Well. I'm just a bit worried about Fran.' She glanced over to another table, where a witch was watching *Cooking for Tiny People* on a spoon. Zarkle was presenting. 'Fran's not on *Cooking for Tiny People*? And she hasn't been seen flying around the city screaming? That's strange.'

'I'm worried about her, too,' Peggy said, taking a sip of her Clutterbucks. 'She was quite upset about the new fairy.'

'I just have a weird feeling …' Tiga began. She placed a hand on the page with the witch-sized Fran dressed like a princess in a jelly castle.

Felicity Bat cackled and nearly fell off her chair.

'WHAT?' Peggy demanded.

Tiga winced. She'd completely forgotten Felicity Bat's new thing was to read minds. As if impressive long-distance levitating wasn't enough!

Felicity Bat could barely speak between the cackles. 'She … thinks … ha!'

'Tiga, do you want to tell us?' Peggy said, kicking Felicity Bat under the table.

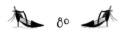

Tiga shook her head.

'She's worried Fran is really out there somewhere, trapped in a jelly castle! Oh, and like the book says, she's witch-sized and dressed as a princess!' Felicity Bat said with utter glee.

Silence engulfed the table.

Tiga looked at each of them. Except for Lucy, they were all trying not to burst out laughing. Fluffanora was pretending to be interested in the huge neon Clutterbucks sign, biting the side of her mouth. Felicity Bat was smirking and Peggy was puffing out her cheeks, which Tiga knew was trademark Peggy Trying Not to Laugh™.

'You're all mean!' Tiga said, throwing her hands in the air and ungracefully slipping off her chair.

'I am your number one fan and I agree!' Lucy shouted. 'Fran is probably trapped in a jelly castle!'

The witches at the next table giggled.

Felicity Bat stared intently at Lucy Tatty. 'Fascinating. Her mind is completely filled with Witch Wars trivia.'

'YOU'RE BORING!' Lucy Tatty roared in Felicity Bat's face.

Tiga held Lucy Tatty by the backpack as she tried to lunge at Felicity Bat, her fists flailing. 'You've got to admit it's weird a picture of Fran appeared in the book and now she's missing.'

'We don't even know she's missing,' Felicity Bat said dismissively. 'We just haven't seen her in a few days. She's in a huff because Peggy said no, she wouldn't squash or imprison Zarkle. She's probably hiding on purpose, to get attention.'

'Fran would *never* –' Tiga stopped. 'Actually, Fran would do that. But I want to know that she's definitely not trapped in a jelly castle.'

Felicity Bat picked up her Clutterbucks drink. 'Suit yourself.'

Mrs Clutterbuck wandered over and stuck a finger in the cake, scooping up some of the icing. 'Heard you mention Fran. There's a fairy outside shouting that Fran's gone missing. Did you know?'

'WHAT?' Tiga cried, racing for the door.

'Wait for me!' Lucy Tatty called after her before turning to Mrs Clutterbuck and thrusting her necklace

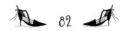

of shrivelled heads up at her. 'Will you sign a shrivelled head? I didn't make one of you because you weren't that important in Witch Wars, were you?'

'LUCY!' Tiga cried. 'PUT DOWN THE SHRIVELLED HEADS.'

Lucy slowly placed the shrivelled heads on the counter as Mrs Clutterbuck eyed her suspiciously. 'In your own time,' Lucy said quietly before cantering out of the door.

14

Please Take a Flyer, Thank You

Outside, standing on the pavement directly below a large dripping pipe, stood a messy and mangled fairy.

'Please take a flyer, thank you, I'm looking for my lost friend. Please take a flyer, thank you, I'm looking for my lost friend.'

Crispy stopped as a particularly large drop of water hit her head from the pipe above. She sidestepped to the left, shook the little soaked flyers in her hand and continued.

'Please take a flyer, thank you, I'm looking for my lost friend. Please take a flyer, thank you.'

Witches were streaming past Crispy, either completely ignoring her or looking at her with disdain. Her matted and wild hair was half stuck to her face.

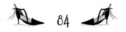

'Please take a flyer, thank you, I'm looking for my lost frie–' A witch accidentally kicked her, sending her flyers soaring into the air. The little ball of mulch tried to leap up and catch them as they fell.

Tiga darted across the street to where Crispy was standing.

'Have you seen Fran?' she asked.

Lucy Tatty caught up with her. 'Argh, it's the evil fairy from Witch Wars!'

'I'm perfectly pleasant,' Crispy said, bent nose in the air. 'And no, Tiga. She is *missing*.'

She handed Tiga a tiny flyer.

'Fran would've loved to see so many pieces of paper with her face on it,' Tiga said glumly, handing one to Lucy, who looked confused.

'I made these flyers to find her. I've checked everywhere – her caravan, Brew's, that little all-you-can-eat Fairy Feast restaurant on Ritzy Lane that she always denies she likes, *all* her hairdressers. It's like she's vanished. Patricia the producer said she couldn't present *Cooking for Tiny People. Zarkle* instead, she

85

said. So Fran left. I thought she was going to come back and kill us all! But she didn't … and then I got worried.'

Tiga opened the book and began flicking to the Fran page to show Crispy. 'I found this book and I'm worried that –' She gasped and dropped it on the ground.

A new page had appeared. A loose page. A *letter*.

It detached from the book and floated to the ground.

TIGA LETTER: Third (third!) attempt to get in touch with Tiga.

WISH YOU COULD GET YOUR FRIEND, WHO WAS ONCE A FAIRY BUT IS NOW A WITCH-SIZED PRINCESS IN A JELLY CASTLE, BACK?

You saw our book - you know that WE CAN MAKE YOUR WISHES COME TRUE.

VISIT THE KARENS! Take the Sinkville

```
Express to the Badlands and follow signs
for:
    The Jelly Castle,
    Boulder Boulevard -
    access via Entrance C.

No hot water bottles, thank you.
```

'We need to speak to Gloria Tatty,' Tiga said urgently, her hand shaking.

'ABSOLUTELY ANYTHING FOR YOU, WE CAN GO TO RAINBOW BONES TO SEE HER RIGHT NOW!' Lucy Tatty roared. She stopped and raised a finger. 'But *why* do we need to speak to Granny?'

Tiga looked down at the book. 'Because this book is spooky and seems to know something, and I want to know what the froglollipops is going on.'

15

Massive Face

A few minutes later, Peggy lifted Crispy from the
pavement and gave the fairy a cuddle.

'WATCH THE MINI BONES! THE MINI
BONES!'

'Sorry,' Peggy said, awkwardly tossing the fairy from
one hand to the other before placing her back on the
ground. 'We'll take care of this, Crispy. I'll make more
MISSING posters and we'll put one in the next *Ritzy
City Post*.'

Crispy was picking her nose and crying. 'Front page?'

Peggy nodded.

Crispy snotted all over the floor. 'And make Fran's
face huge?'

'Will do,' Peggy said patiently.

Felicity Bat patted the little fairy on the back with a look of mild disgust. 'We'll find her, and everything will be … what's the word she loves? *Oh yes*, fabulous. Everything will be fabulous again.'

16

Spellbooks and Dust

RITZY CITY POST

ZARKLE OPENS MAVIS'S NEW JAM (AND SOMETIMES CATS) STALL!

Zarkle has just opened Mavis's new stall after it was crushed by a falling Sinkville Express carriage this morning. Her refurbished stall will sell her usual seven hundred varieties of jam, and one variety of cat, and now her latest thing: cat-shaped jam jars.

We asked Zarkle if she eats jam and she said –

Unfortunately our reporter rushed off to a dentist appointment and didn't finish – or indeed practically start – the interview.

Crispy thrust the article up to Felicity Bat as soon as the door to Linden House opened. 'Where is Fran's gigantic face, then?'

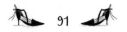

Felicity Bat urgently flicked through the paper. 'She's, well, not *front* page …'

Crispy scrunched up her already scrunched-up nose. 'Zarkle opening Mavis's jam stall is front page.'

Peggy came racing to the door and skidded to a halt.

'But … but … oh, look,' Felicity Bat went on. 'Here Fran is, page forty, next to this article on How to Get Dust off Spellbooks.'

'How do you get dust off spellbooks?' Peggy asked.

Crispy put her head in her tiny claw-like hands and sighed.

Felicity Bat held the paper close to her nose and scanned the article. 'You blow on them.'

17

Rainbow Bones

Tiga stood at the base of a rainbow-coloured tower, smack bang in the middle of all the tall turrets that made up the Towers area of Sinkville. She hadn't been back since Witch Wars, and seeing Lucy skipping around dressed like her was making her feel woozy.

Lucy Tatty knocked on the door, just below a sign that read RAINBOW BONES! Instantly, the door was whipped open and an efficient-looking witch with a long face and whirring eyes ushered them up some rainbow-coloured stairs and into a long, wide room – an impossibility given the tower was tall and thin. Tiga was about to ask how the room could possibly be so long when she spotted the decorations – hundreds of rainbow-coloured skeletons dancing up and down the walls.

An old witch poked her head out into the hallway and shouted, 'HELLO, CATS!'

'A rainbow skeleton is a symbol of advanced dancing,' Lucy Tatty said, as she trotted down the corridor. 'Only exceptionally talented witches are chosen to attend

Rainbow Bones, the most respected Sinkville dance group! You need to be at least one hundred. It's the minimum age. A lot of the witches here are over four hundred years old, and excellent at high kicks.'

Tiga laughed as Lucy Tatty held a finger to her lips. 'They're in here, but they might be practising.'

They *were* practising. A line of ancient witches all charging from left to right on a stage, doing high kicks so fast their legs were just swipes of colour staining the air.

'AH, IT'S MY GRANDDAUGHTER AND A STRANGER,' a beautiful old woman with glossy hair down to her knees squealed, leg-kicking her way over to them, completely disrupting the routine.

Tiga felt her cheeks stinging as all the witches stared at her – a mix of curiosity and anger. How dare these young witches interrupt them?!

'That's my gran,' Lucy Tatty whispered, and the witch stopped kicking in front of them.

'Granny! Look, I've got a new friend. This is Tiga,' Lucy said, squeezing Tiga's arm. 'FROM WITCH WARS.'

Tiga was distracted by another old witch shyly leg-kicking her way past them. Her hair was tied up in two loose buns on either side of her head.

'Is she your friend?' Tiga asked Gloria Tatty, who was watching the old witch leg-kick her way out of the room.

'Who? Her? No … I don't have any friends,' Gloria Tatty said.

'Not one?' Lucy Tatty asked.

'Well, I have *one*. But he lives far, far away.'

'I'm glad Tiga doesn't live far, far away,' Lucy Tatty prattled on. 'Because now I can ask her questions about her, her life and Witch Wars ALL THE TIME! Because I am Tiga's number one fan.'

Tiga smiled weakly.

Gloria Tatty blinked at them. 'Tea?' she finally asked. Tiga nodded eagerly as Gloria Tatty ushered them to the corner of the room, where there was a rickety old table with just the right amount of cups and saucers.

Tiga stared at Gloria Tatty, trying to figure her out. She looked more stern than in her photo. More serious. Certainly more serious than you'd imagine the witch who wrote a story about a girl eating a *broom* would be. Her head was tilted slightly to the side, like an inquisitive dog, but with piercing eyes that displayed all the calculation and cunning of a cat. She was pleasant enough, but Tiga could sense she was nervous, like she knew what they had come to speak to her about.

'Gran,' Lucy said, wasting no time. 'We found this.'

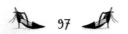

She pointed at Tiga, and on cue, Tiga plonked *The Karens* down on the table.

Gloria Tatty remained stiff in her seat and stared at it.

'It keeps updating,' Tiga explained. 'It shows Fran the fairy in it and a letter addressed to me fell from it, inviting me to visit The Karens.'

Gloria Tatty lifted it in the air. Tiga could see her hands were shaking slightly. She sniffed the book, her eyes closed.

'Is the book special?' Tiga asked.

'You're special,' Lucy Tatty oozed, punching Tiga's arm.

Tiga watched as Gloria Tatty placed it back on the table and nudged its edge, adjusting it so it was sitting perfectly square. 'Never seen that book my life,' she lied.

'It does say you wrote it,' Tiga pointed out.

Gloria Tatty shrugged and slid it off the table, tucking it under her arm. 'I'm keeping it.'

'No,' Tiga said, trying to grab it.

'GET OFF!' Gloria Tatty shouted, as Tiga snatched the book and charged down the corridor.

'Wait, Tiga!' Lucy Tatty cried.

She looked back. Behind a galloping Lucy was Gloria Tatty, staring at Tiga. 'YOU MUST NOT TRUST THE BOOK!' came the echo of Gloria Tatty's shrill scream, following Tiga down the stairs and out of the door. 'PUT IT BACK WHERE YOU FOUND IT, TIGA. IT'S DANGEROUS!'

18

Massive Face, Part 2

'Crispy …' Felicity Bat said, levitating outside Linden House. 'What are you doing?'

Crispy slopped paint across the front of Linden House. 'Finished!' she said as she flew back a bit to admire her handiwork. There, smack bang on the Linden House building, was a giant picture of Fran's face. 'This is even BETTER than the front page of the *Ritzy City Post*,' she said, rubbing her hands together with glee.

'Did you get permission from Peggy to do this, Crispy?' Felicity Bat asked, as Crispy scrawled MISSING across Fran's forehead.

'Nope,' Crispy said.

Peggy tripped and fell out of the doorway. 'Oh, hello, Crispy! What's going on out here?'

She spotted the giant sloppy Fran face painted on the front of the building.

'Ah.'

'She said she didn't get permission from you,' Felicity Bat said, smirking at Crispy.

Peggy stood for a moment taking it in. 'You know, Crispy –'

'Pun-ish her,' Felicity Bat said in an excited whisper.

'You know, Crispy,' Peggy started again, shooting Felicity Bat a look. 'I think it's … SPECTACULAR! Well done.'

'Spectacular,' Crispy mouthed at Felicity Bat, flashing her a wonky, smug grin.

19

Uh-Oh ...

'Why did you do that?' Lucy Tatty panted as she caught up with Tiga. 'Because you're amazing and you have a plan, I'm sure, but I have to ask.'

Tiga opened the book again to reassure herself that she wasn't going insane. The big princess in the jelly castle was unmistakably Fran, just a bigger version. She sighed, closed the book and handed it to Lucy.

There's only one thing left to do, she thought, taking the piece of paper out of her pocket. She ran a finger over the last paragraph.

VISIT THE KARENS! Take the Sinkville Express to the Badlands and follow signs for:

```
The Jelly Castle,
Boulder Boulevard -
access via Entrance C.
```

```
No hot water bottles, thank you.
```

She folded it up and stashed it back in her pocket.

'What are we doing now, Tig*amazing*?' Lucy asked. 'That's my new name for you, by the way.'

'I've got to find out what's happened to Fran, Lucy. I'm going to the Badlands.'

☆⭐☆

Before Tiga knew what she was doing, she and Lucy were on the Sinkville Express heading straight for the Badlands. Even if the whole thing turned out to be some sort of elaborate joke and she was about to make a complete fool of herself, Tiga still wanted to know Fran was safe. Now all she had to do was convince Lucy to get off at Silver City without her.

'Next stop, Silver City!'

Tiga turned to Lucy and smiled. 'I know, let's *race* home.'

'AMAZING IDEA, TIGAMAZING!'

(Five minutes later.)

'No, *you* get out of the carriage first.'

'No, Lucy, *you* first.'

'But you were in Witch Wars, I insist *you* go first.'

Tiga tried to push Lucy out of the carriage, but the train began to move.

'Next stop, THE BADLANDS.'

'Great,' Tiga groaned as the train trundled out of Silver City station.

'Oh no,' Lucy Tatty said. 'We missed our stop!' She reached into her bag and pulled out a little book. 'Do you want to do some drawing? I just got this new Witch Wars activity book. It's called *Draw Awful Clothes on Aggie Hoof, for Fun.*'

'Lucy!' Tiga cried, taking the book and tossing it

over the edge of the carriage. 'I was planning to go to the Badlands. Now you'll have to come with me.'

Lucy Tatty thought for a moment. 'AN ADVENTURE! Although, whoa, it will be a scary one because no one knows what's in the Badlands. But you're a hero so I feel completely safe.' She nuzzled into Tiga's arm.

'What?' Tiga cried. 'No one knows what's in the Badlands?'

'No one really talks about the Badlands,' Lucy said cheerily. 'At school they teach us that the Badlands in the olden days was the stronghold of terrible witches, a place of strange beasts and unimaginable spells. If you look at any map of Sinkville, it just shows a vast expanse of land and a little witch shrugging in the middle of it.'

Tiga pulled the Karens' letter from her pocket. 'I wonder why this letter gives an address in the Badlands ...'

'Oh! Oh! Oh!' Lucy Tatty said, rummaging around in her backpack. 'That reminds me. This floated into my hand outside Clutterbucks.'

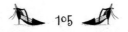

DO YOU WISH YOU WERE TIGA OR AT THE
VERY LEAST SORT OF ATTACHED TO HER
SIDE ALL THE TIME, FOR EVER?

You saw our book - you know that
WE CAN MAKE YOUR WISHES COME TRUE
(not like a genie, we're better than
that rubbish).

VISIT THE KARENS! Take the Sinkville
Express to the Badlands and follow signs
for:
    The Jelly Castle,
    Boulder Boulevard -
    access via Entrance C.

No really hot soups, please.

She looked adoringly at Tiga. 'That would be my
wish.'

    Tiga shifted uncomfortably in her seat. The carriage

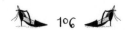

groaned and creaked. 'So the Karens send these letters to lots of witches. Maybe they sent Fran a letter, too. Maybe you make a wish and then they trap you in the Jelly Castle. Maybe the Karens are awful Badlands witches …'

'I don't think they'd live in a jelly castle if they were awful …' Lucy Tatty said as the train passed a tattered sign limply floating in the air: THE BADLANDS. 'After all, jelly is delicious. I wonder if any of the others have received letters.'

The wind was picking up and the Sinkville Express carriages rattled, their creaking joints whispering, *USE ANOTHER MODE OF TRANSPORT, ANYTHING BUT US.*

And that's when Tiga noticed the jam lining the far edge of the carriage. 'Lucy,' she said slowly, grabbing the side of the carriage as it groaned louder. 'The jam … it's the same carriage we were in on our way to Ritzy City. The one that fe–'

The carriage gave a final groan and fell from the tracks.

'I KNEW IT!' Tiga screamed,
as they spiralled down
and down into
the darkness
below.

20

The Karens Underestimate Fluffanora

Fluffanora was finishing up her Clutterbucks cocktail when a piece of paper floated on to the table.

DO YOU WISH YOU COULD BEWITCH YOUR
CAT, MRS PUMPKIN, SO SHE IS MASSIVE,
WITH WINGS, AND THEN YOU COULD FLY
ABOUT ON HER BACK?

You saw our book - you know that
WE CAN MAKE YOUR WISHES COME TRUE
(not like a genie, we're better than
that rubbish).

VISIT THE KARENS! Take the Sinkville Express to the Badlands and follow signs for:
    The Jelly Castle,
    Boulder Boulevard -
    access via Entrance C.

No filled kettles, you hear.

'Idiots,' Fluffanora said, ripping the piece of paper into tiny pieces. 'That's what I wanted *yesterday*.'

21

But No One Goes to the Badlands ...

Tiga grabbed frantically at the darkness. 'Lucy!' she cried, her voice echoing in the foggy expanse.

THUD!

THUMP!

Tiga landed on what felt like a sponge, and then Lucy fell on her head.

She rubbed her eyes. Lucy Tatty was already back on her feet, running from left to right, screaming, 'I've got a scrape! I've got a scrape!'

As Tiga tried to calm her down, the carriage wobbled and floated back up to the track, reattaching itself before speeding off.

Tiga waved her fists at it. 'THANKS A LOT!'

Lucy frantically felt around on the ground. 'My

backpack!' she shouted. 'I CAN'T FIND MY BACKPACK!' Cradling her scraped arm, she darted off into the black abyss beyond.

Tiga scrambled to her feet and chased after her. 'Lucy! Stop! It might be dangerous!'

A smog began to swirl around them, as if to say, OH, THIS IS DANGEROUS ALL RIGHT.

Special Effects

'Karen, darling, that's enough of the smog machine, it looks really eerie now,' said Tall Karen, hitting the OFF button and shoving the contraption out of the way.

'What do you think about ghost noises, darling, or random bird tweets?' said Smog Machine Karen.

'I think we are *witches*, not ghosts *or* birds, and you are taking this too far, darling.'

Smog Machine Karen hung her head. 'But witches aren't scary, darling, ghosts are. Maybe some fairy ghosts at least? Would be quite a nice fit, given we got the fairy Fran. Freak them out a bit, darling? I know a spell for ghost fairies …'

Tall Karen rubbed her forehead. 'If you must,' she said, faintly.

23

Who Switched the Smog Off?

The smog vanished almost as quickly as it had appeared. Like someone had switched it off, Tiga thought …

Onwards they went, their eyes adjusting to the darkness as they ventured further into the Badlands. Tiga spotted it first. Wobbling amongst the mountainous terrain and spindly smog-coated trees was a jelly castle with so many turrets and tiny windows it looked like you could squish every single witch in Sinkville inside it.

Tiga looked at the little note the Karens had sent her. *Access via Entrance C.*

She squeezed Lucy Tatty's arm. 'Ready?'

Lucy Tatty shrugged. 'I'm just following you, because I am –'

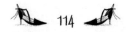

'Your number one fan,' Tiga said.

'No,' Lucy said. 'I'm not wearing my contact lenses.'

The bridge was made of jelly and peppered with gigantic jelly statues of witches in elaborate hats reclining and eating cakes.

Tiga held up the book. 'These must be the Karens, in jelly statue form,' she said, showing Lucy the cover of the book. 'See, they look the same.'

'They don't look scary …' Lucy Tatty said, staring up at one that was dangling a French fancy over her gaping mouth. 'I don't think anyone who likes cakes can be terrible. You never see a baddie eating a chocolate eclair, do you?'

The bridge wobbled as they walked but it was surprisingly sturdy, like walking on a reliable trampoline.

'WHAT'S BACK THERE?' Lucy Tatty cried, grabbing her arm.

Tiga looked behind them. There was nothing but darkness.

She put her arm around Lucy's shoulder. 'Nothing. Everything is fine.'

Only it wasn't fine. They were walking towards a jelly castle that contained a bunch of witches, all called Karen, who may or may not have turned Fran into a large princess thing.

As the bridge curved, Tiga could see jiggling jelly walls flanking the castle, with perfectly pruned jelly hedges peeking over the top. Beneath the bridge a bubbling jelly moat slopped its way along, but Tiga had no idea where it went. She couldn't see where the castle walls ended. They seemed to stretch for miles.

The elaborate towers wobbled overhead as they got closer. Tiga couldn't tell if the bridge had begun to shake more or if it was Lucy Tatty trembling under her arm.

'Almost there …' Tiga whispered.

An ornate jelly gate up ahead opened, revealing a quivering wall of doors.

'I bet we'll just go in, eat some cake, make wishes and then go home and stay alive!' Lucy Tatty rambled.

Fran's Big Feet

'TIGA! IT'S ME!' Fran yelled from the highest jelly turret of them all. 'IT'S YOUR FABULOUS FAIRY, TIGA!'

But Tiga couldn't hear her.

'AREN'T I FABULOUS NOW! LOOK – WITCH-SIZED FEET AND SHOES TO MATCH!' She kicked the jelly turret, sending a clump of the stuff soaring down to Lucy, who spotted it and gulped, keeping her eyes firmly fixed on it.

'WITCH WARS SUPERFAN!' Fran cried, pointing a finger at Lucy. 'THAT WAS ME!'

But Lucy couldn't hear her.

A slender arm reached out from a hatch in the door and unfurled a spindly finger. 'Come in, darlings.'

Fran peered as far over the edge of the turret window as she could manage before her vertigo set in. 'TIGA! LUCY! THAT'S THE WRONG WAY!'

But it was too late; they were already inside.

25

Inside That Jelly Castle

'Quickly, quickly inside, no dilly-dallying,' said a witch clad in a dress that looked a lot like a black trifle, her perfectly round face resembling a nice little cherry on the top.

Tiga reluctantly obeyed. The witch snatched the piece of paper out of her hand.

'Ah, you're here for wishes. KAAAARRRREEEEN!' she roared.

'Are … are … *you* not Karen?' Lucy Tatty stammered.

'Oh, we're all Karens, darling,' she said, bending down and adding in a whisper, 'But some of us are much better than others.'

A nervous-looking witch in an equally elaborate but altogether different outfit came clattering through the

door. Her dress was completely plain and slim fitting until it got to the shoulders, where the fabric ballooned in huge theatrical lumps.

'INVADERS!' she roared when she spotted the witches. Lucy dived behind Tiga and hid her face.

'No, no, you balloon,' Trifle Karen snapped. 'They are wishers.'

'Wishers!' Balloon-Shoulders Karen squealed. 'Oh, darling, now I can get the Unicorn Yoga Instructor I wanted!'

Trifle Karen pushed her out of the way. '*No*, darling. Darling, we agreed we would get the Soothing Shark Spa, like I said the other day, darling.'

Balloon-Shoulders Karen shook her head furiously. '*NO*, you said, darling, the sharks could be dangerous.'

'They do a sort of deep sea massage, the sharks. Darling, it's meant to be excellent for the skin.'

Balloon-Shoulders Karen shook her head again, even more furiously this time. 'Darling, you definitely said you couldn't guarantee the sharks wouldn't take a break from massaging and gobble us … darling.'

Tiga and Lucy turned their heads, back and forth from one Karen to the other, like two little witches watching an incredibly odd, nonsensical tennis match.

'And darling, Cheese Grater Karen will be livid if she doesn't get her cheese grater.'

'SHE DOESN'T EVEN HAVE ANY CHEESE, DARLING!' Trifle Karen roared. 'AND SHE ALREADY HAS ONE!'

'Darling, I think she just likes holding the cheese grater, darling. Wants one for each hand now, darling.'

Trifle Karen turned towards Tiga and Lucy, a strained smile smacked on her tiny, cherry-like face. 'Now, my darlings, I believe you want to make a wish …'

Balloon-Shoulders Karen sighed and walked towards a large door at the back of the room. 'Follow me.'

'We actually just want to find our friend,' Tiga said, remaining rooted to the spot. 'Fran? The fairy? Now witch-sized?'

Trifle Karen snaked closer. 'Is that your wish? Did you say wish?'

'No,' Tiga said quietly. 'I don't think I did …'

Trifle Karen muttered something Tiga couldn't quite hear, but she sounded croaky and annoyed. 'She's just through here, darlings.'

And so Tiga followed, as Lucy pulled on her dress and muttered, 'I don't want to be in this jelly castle any more. I want to be back in shimmering Silver City.'

They strolled past elaborate paintings and grotesque sculptures and stomped past doors marked with 'Large Cinema, Darling', 'Bowling Alley, Darling', 'Largest Collection of Dragon Costumes, Darling'.

Tiga stopped at that one and blinked.

Trifle Karen rolled her eyes. 'That's Karen's fault.'

Tiga looked at Balloon-Shoulders Karen.

'No, not that Karen, darling,' said Trifle Karen, pointing at Balloon-Shoulders Karen. 'Another Karen.'

Onwards they went, into a vast hallway with a sweeping jelly staircase studded with gems. There was a slide running along beside it.

'Is that a *real* slide?' Lucy Tatty asked eagerly.

Trifle Karen rolled her eyes. 'Yes, that's what Karen

wanted. Waste of a wish, *ahem*, I mean a waste of *time* if you ask me.'

'She wished for it?' Tiga asked.

'Not exactly,' Trifle Karen said, leading them down a corridor lined with cakes – eight-tiered monsters covered in cream and delicious jam.

'Why is your castle made of jelly?' Lucy Tatty asked.

'Darling, why not!'

'How many Karens live in this place?' Tiga asked as Trifle Karen put her hand on her shoulder and gently pushed her further down the corridor.

'Thirteen, darling. Like I said, some better than others.'

They rounded a corner and bumped into another Karen, whose neck was plastered with chunky, gem-covered chains. She was clutching a pair of kicking tights.

'Dennis!' Tiga gasped.

'What is that?' Trifle Karen asked.

Jewel-Covered Karen tied Dennis in a knot and threw him on the ground.

'Found it trying to steal the jewels on the staircase,' she called back.

'Crazy, darling,' Trifle Karen said dismissively, ushering them on.

Tiga leaned back, quickly scooped Dennis up and put him in her skirt pocket.

'TIGAMAZING,' Lucy's voice boomed, making the jelly wobble. 'WHAT DID YOU JUST PU–'

'Sssh,' Tiga said, smiling meekly at the Karens.

26

At the Mmmf

Peggy stood in the middle of the mess that was the Mmmf (the Ministry of Mess and Many Files) in Pearl Peak, her nose in a book. 'There *must* be a way to stop that Sinkville Express carriage falling off the tracks.'

Tina Gloop, the rickety old witch in charge of the Mmmf, came sliding down the stairs with more documents. 'It was always breaking in my day – rarely had a successful journey, if I remember correctly. And even then a carriage always fell off, especially around the Badlands. I don't know why that engineer Lucinda Bunch insisted on building it so it took that route. No one ever has or ever will go there!'

'At least no one stays in the carriage for that bit of the

track,' Peggy said. 'They all get off at Silver City. That's the last stop before the train loops around the Badlands and comes back. What's worrying me is that the carriage fell off over Ritzy City the other day.'

Felicity Bat levitated into the room, flicking papers with her fingers. 'Just got another report of the carriage falling off, this time around the Badlands.'

'At least it was the Badlands, so no one was on the train,' Peggy said, picking up another stack of papers.

'Well …' Felicity Bat began.

'But there wasn't anyone in the carriage, was there?' Peggy asked, as Felicity Bat held up a familiar-looking red-stained backpack.

Peggy screamed. 'Is that BLOOD!?'

'No,' Felicity Bat said, licking it and making Peggy wince. 'It's just jam. Probably still there from when the carriage fell on Mavis's jam stall.'

Peggy's eyes fixed on the backpack. 'I recognise that – oh FROGSTICKS!'

'No one says frogsticks any more,' Felicity Bat said. 'It's frogacinos now.'

'In my day,' Tina Gloop said shakily, 'we just said frogancienttimes.'

'Tiga must have been in that carriage with Lucy,' Peggy said, running towards the door and smacking into a stack of files. 'She wouldn't go to the Badlands without good reason – she must be searching for the jelly castle in that book she found.'

Felicity Bat cackled. 'She's gone properly insa–' She stopped and cocked her head to the side. 'What hidden file?' she asked, floating slowly towards Tina Gloop.

Tina Gloop gasped and took a step back. 'Whu? I didn't say anything!'

Peggy snapped the book shut and looked at her. 'Hidden file?'

'How are you doing that? No, no, I didn't say anything. I was just … thinking …'

Peggy pointed her finger at Felicity Bat, who hung her head and levitated lower. 'I told you about that, Felicity! No mind reading!'

'MIND READING?!' Tina Gloop gasped. 'I suppose

you are the best witch we've had for ages, but almost *no one* can do that.'

'You don't need to mind read all the time,' Peggy went on.

'Just a bit of practice,' Felicity Bat whispered out of the corner of her mouth, eyes firmly fixed on the floor.

'No!' Peggy said. 'No mind reading.'

'But she did find out about my hidden file,' Tina Gloop said.

'True,' Peggy said. 'What is that?'

Tina Gloop trotted over to the wall and kicked it. The peeling wallpaper fell away to reveal a tunnel. She trotted through while Peggy and Felicity Bat stared at each other. 'A long time ago, Lucinda Bunch asked me to hide this file in the safest place in the Mmmf. Paid me *so many sinkels* to do it, too. I completely forgot about it until you marched in here and mentioned her. Silly old memory.'

Peggy coughed as Tina Gloop emerged from the tunnel in a cloud of dust.

'She wanted to make sure this was safe – she said

something like "Someone might need it one day …" All eerie she said it, too.' She handed Felicity Bat the tattered old notebook.

'Anything interesting?' Peggy asked, wiping the dust off her glasses with her fingers, as if they were windscreen wipers.

Felicity Bat's eyebrows knitted together. She was deep in thought.

'What is it?' Peggy asked.

'I don't believe it, Pegs. The book. The weird Karens book Tiga keeps going on about.'

'What about it?'

Felicity Bat held up the notebook. 'It seems Lucinda Bunch knew about that book too. And she believed it was extremely dangerous.'

To the Hall of Swings

'In here, we have the Great Hall of Swings, darlings. SWINGS.'

Tiga held on to the jiggling jelly wall and peered into the room. Swings, like the kind you would find in parks and people's back gardens in the world above the pipes, were fixed to the ceiling. Hundreds of them.

'SWIIIIIINGS!' Lucy Tatty cried. Tiga grabbed the young witch's dress before she could dart into the room.

'Why do you have a room filled with swings?'

Trifle Karen and Balloon-Shoulders Karen looked at each other.

'Karen, darling,' they said.

'Another Karen?' Tiga asked.

They both nodded and rolled their eyes.

That was when Tiga heard it.

'HAS THERE BEEN ANYONE
MORE FABULOUS EVER?
NOPEDY NOPE.
FRAN, FRAN, FOR EVER.'

It was slightly deeper and less screechy than she was used to, but it was the same fabulous, slightly annoying, unmistakable tone of …

'FRAN!' Tiga cried, racing through the swing room, batting the things out of the way as she went. 'FRAN!'

'WAIT!' the Karens cried, charging after her. 'You need to make a wish first, darling. A WISH!'

Lucy watched them go and then sneakily slid on to a swing.

☆☆☆

Tiga charged up some curling jelly steps, her heart firmly fixed in her mouth. She didn't know whether she was going to roar with delight or be really sick. 'FRAN!' she cried again. 'I'M COMING!'

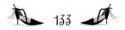

Suddenly the jelly steps stopped and she went
ploughing into a small jelly door. She took a step back,
the squidgy sound of the Karens' feet just moments
behind her.

She curled her hand into a fist and stood with it
suspended in front of the door. 'Only, you can't really
knock on jelly,' she said out loud.

'WHAT?' came Fran's voice from inside.

'Fran, let me in!'

'Oh, Tiga, you made it to my turret! How WON-DERFUL,' she said, throwing open the door.

Tiga couldn't believe her eyeballs. There she was – Fran! Only now she was the exact same height as Tiga, if you didn't count the beehive, which made her twice as tall.

'It's true! You're *witch-sized*.'

Fran nodded. 'Isn't it FABULOUS? And I'm a princess, you see.' She twirled around.

Tiga sighed. 'Well, lucky I got here in time. I'm here to rescue you, princess.'

'Oh, just like a fairy tale! ONLY I'M NOT A *FAIRY* IN THE FAIRY TALE,' Fran rambled. 'I'm a witch-sized princess.'

'Yes,' Tiga groaned.

'Also, it's not like a fairy tale because I don't want to leave.'

'WHAT?' Tiga said, as a clump of Karens she'd never seen before trotted into the turret.

Suitcases

Ritzy City's just-opened Sinkville Express station was a big old bag of bustle – hundreds of witches filed in and out of the magically rotating turnstiles, all stamped with the glittering letters R.C. There was a hatch in the wall dispensing Clutterbucks drinks, with witches in front of it shouting things like, 'One We Hate Celia Crayfish cocktail, please!', and a row of carts selling things for the journey, from shiny new books and stacks of crinkled *Toad* magazines to jam and some very old hats.

'OLD WITCH HATS WOT GOT STUCK IN THE PIPES! GET YOUR OLD WITCH HATS!'

'It's the cart witch,' Peggy whispered as Felicity

Bat grabbed a couple of tickets floating through the air.

That's how the tickets worked – they'd fly around in a formation that was an exact replica of the Sinkville Express route, and witches jumped to grab a ticket. The route looked a lot like the shape of a lollipop with a kink in it – an almost straight line, running from Pearl Peak to Brollywood to the Towers across to the Docks (that was the kink), then to Ritzy City, Driptown and Silver City before doing a loop around the Badlands back to Silver City, where it would do the whole route backwards, all the way back to Pearl Peak.

'I don't get it,' Peggy said, flipping through the note-book. 'Lucinda Bunch was trying to stop the Karens because of their dangerous wishes.'

Felicity Bat nodded. 'It seems the Karens' book, the one Tiga showed us, was once used by other witches, including Lucinda Bunch, to make wishes. Only the wishes have twists. Bad twists.' She pointed at a page in the notebook.

*The Karens can communicate with you and sense
your wish by two methods:*

1. *If you see the Karens' book.*
2. *If you see their jelly castle in the Badlands.*

'And it gets worse,' Felicity Bat said. 'No one ever went
to the Badlands, so the second one was never really an
option for the Karens.'

'We should've listened to Tiga,' Peggy said quietly.

Felicity Bat stuck her nose in the air. 'She's rarely right.'

'Wait a second,' Peggy asked, her face a mangle of
scrunched nose and confusion. 'Why would Lucinda
Bunch build a railway that went over the Badlands if she
knew that if a witch saw the jelly castle, the Karens
would be able to get to them?'

Felicity Bat took the notebook and flipped a couple
of pages back. 'Because that was Lucinda Bunch's wish.
She saw the book, wished for the railway.' She tapped a
sketch on the page of a railway track, but this one only
went as far as Silver City, not into the Badlands.

'And the Karens' twist was to extend the track into the Badlands,' Peggy said.

'And look at this,' Felicity Bat said, pulling a loose document from the notebook. 'Remember Tina Gloop told you the railway kept breaking back then, too? That the same carriage always fell off? Lucinda Bunch says here it was a spell the Karens put on it. She tried to figure out how to reverse the spell, but couldn't.'

Peggy looked expectantly at Felicity Bat.

'I'll do my best,' she said, folding the paper carefully and slipping it in her pocket.

☆⭐☆

They stepped out on to the platform and found the Sinkville Express waiting for them. Up ahead, in the driver's carriage, a thin ribbon of glittery steam twisted in the air.

'ALL ABOARD! ANY BAGS LEFT UNATTENDED WILL BE GIVEN A RIGHT OLD TELLING OFF!'

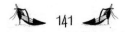

A couple of bags wiggled their way from the platform into a carriage.

'I really need to get myself one of those self-walking suitcases,' Peggy said, watching them go.

'A load of old toad, if you ask me,' Felicity Bat said. 'They've got minds of their own – and they're arrogant.'

They watched a suitcase open itself up and use its handle to pour in a glass of Clutterbucks, as if it was actually drinking it.

The witch next to it winced. 'Soaked clothes, *again*. Thank you, suitcase …'

'A suitcase with a mind of its own, how wonderful!' Peggy said, as Felicity Bat rolled her eyes.

'I have a bad feeling about today,' Felicity Bat said, her long, spindly fingers twitching at her sides. 'And I am an expert in bad.'

'Everything will be just fine,' Peggy assured herself as she marched towards the carriage. 'As long as Tiga doesn't make a wish.'

29

All of Them

The Karens assembled in front of Tiga and witch-sized Fran. They were a hotchpotch of tall and small, all in structured black dresses, smiling sweetly. Tiga looked at each of them, counting as she went.

Eleven, twelve …

'I thought you said there were thirteen of you,' she said.

The Karen in the middle, who was clad in a gorgeous sparkling dress and an even more sparkling cloak – the hood up so you could only see her eyes – took a step forward. A cat followed by her spiky shoes.

'Thirteen,' she croaked, pointing at the cat.

'Miaow,' it said.

'Oh, right,' Tiga stuttered, remembering the Karens' book. 'And their cat, also called Karen.'

'I'm Senior Karen,' said the witch, taking off her cloak. She was beautiful, with piercing green eyes that swirled with mystery and a lot of eye juice. 'It's a pleasure to meet you, darling.'

She clicked her fingers, and Trifle Karen handed her a piece of paper.

'Ah, yes. Wants her friend back. Is that your final wish, darling?' she asked, moving closer to Tiga.

'I don't want to go back,' Fran said, folding her arms. 'I thought I wanted to be big so I could hold a jar.'

'What?' Tiga spluttered.

'To trap Zarkle, *obviously*. Put her in the jar, hide her in a fridge.'

'Fran!' Tiga cried. 'That is terrible.'

'I know,' Fran said. 'A terrible plan given someone would probably find her in the fridge.'

'No, Fran, it's terrible because it would be mean.'

Fran stuck her nose in the air. 'Well, it doesn't matter, because now I'm a princess I don't need to capture and hide Zarkle! I have a jelly castle! WHO'S WINNING NOW, ZARKLE?'

Tiga threw her hands in the air. 'What are you going to do in here for ever?'

'Well, um, I'll probably do princess stuff,' Fran said. 'Like sing to birds and … weave things?'

Tiga stared at her.

'Most importantly. I am now the most FABULOUS witch-sized princess in Sinkville.'

Senior Karen took a step forward. 'If we can speed this up, darlings, I'd really appreciate it.'

'You were fabulous just the way you were!' Tiga said, taking Fran's hand and completely ignoring Senior Karen. 'You were my favourite part of Sinkville. You don't need to be bigger, or a princess, or own a jelly castle to be fabulous. You're Fran the Fabulous Fairy! You saved me and brought me here. To me, you are more magical and fabulous than all of Sinkville put together.'

Fran thought about that for a moment. 'Sorry, just going back to nearer the beginning of your fan speech, did you say I was your *favourite* part of Sinkville?'

Tiga nodded.

'Oh, Tiga!' Fran said, leaping on the spot. '*I'M* MY FAVOURITE PART OF SINKVILLE TOO! I'd almost forgotten that. Yes, let's get out of here.'

'Ready to make that wish now?' Senior Karen asked, as all the Karens took an eager step forward.

'No,' Tiga said. 'She wants to come with me, so we'll just be leaving now.'

The Karens clustered around the doorway. Tiga

tried to edge past, but they moved with her, blocking her way.

'I'm afraid you'll have to make a wish, if you want to leave.'

☆⭐☆

'And your wish is done!' Senior Karen said, rubbing her hands together. 'You wished you could leave, and now you can.'

Tiga looked from Senior Karen to Fran. It was bizarre her being so big.

'Felicity Bat will do a shrink spell and you'll be back to normal in no time,' Tiga said, patting Fran firmly on the back.

Senior Karen looked to the other Karens and sniggered. 'Oh yes. A shrink spell.'

Tiga smiled, relieved it was over. 'Well, I'll just go and find Lucy and we'll be on our way.'

One of the Karens raced to the window and squealed. In the distance in the courtyard beyond, a jelly tower was growing out of the ground. Tiga rubbed her eyes.

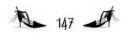

'What is that?' she asked.

'It's expansion, darling!' a Karen with mismatched ears cried. 'My cake tower!'

'Your what?' Tiga asked, but the rest of the Karens were too busy groaning.

'Can't believe you got the cake tower. I only wanted unlimited gold,' said a very short Karen.

'I wanted a room filled with swans,' Tall Karen scoffed.

'I asked for another cheese grater …' said Cheese-Grater Karen.

'What's going on?!' Tiga cried.

Senior Karen, with a swish of her cloak, took a seat on the rickety little chair by the window. 'Every time someone makes a wish with us, darling, we get something for our jelly castle.'

'Oh,' Tiga said.

'We each put a request in a little jelly pot and one is chosen at random, darling. It's really rather exciting. Like a lottery, darling.'

Tiga looked at Fran, who had joined the Karens to

148

watch the growing Cake Tower. 'So what did you get with Fran's wish?'

'A gigantic wardrobe of fabulous cloaks,' Senior Karen said, stroking her cloak adoringly. 'Hundreds and hundreds of them.'

'That's … nice,' Tiga mumbled. 'Right, well, like I said. I'm just going to get Lucy and leave.'

'She's downstairs,' Senior Karen said. 'By the door you came in, Entrance C.'

'CAKE TOWER! CAKE TOWER! CAKE TOWER!' Fran chanted, jumping up and down and high-fiving Mismatched-Ears Karen.

Tiga grabbed Fran's arm and dragged her out of the door as Senior Karen cackled.

'What twist did you put on Tiga's wish?' Smog-Machine Karen asked eagerly.

'They can leave – but only after they complete three impossible tests!' she croaked. 'They will be trapped, the three of them. They'll have to make more wishes to get out!'

'Genius,' Smog-Machine Karen spluttered, stroking Senior Karen's arm adoringly.

Senior Karen grinned. 'Get ready for more expansion, darlings.'

RITZY CITY POST

EXCLUSIVE INTERVIEW

Today our reporter is interviewing Ula Uppington, who lives at No. 4 Ritzy Close. She recently purchased a cat from Mavis's Jam (And Sometimes Cats) Stall, only it wasn't a cat, it was a jam jar *shaped* like a cat. Ula Uppington doesn't know this, and that is *fascinating*.

Reporter: Ula Uppington, please tell us about your new *cat*.
Ula Uppington: He is quiet and as hard as glass and doesn't eat or move.
Reporter: And his name?
Ula Uppington: Cat.

Reporter: Ula Uppington, have you ever owned a cat before?

Ula Uppington: This is my first one.

Reporter: Do you think it's a *normal* cat?

Ula Uppington: Its head screws off. So yes.

Reporter: Isn't that more something that, I don't know, a *jar* would do?

Ula Uppington: Jars don't have tails or names like Cat.

Reporter: Excellent point. I can't even remember what this interview was about.

Ula Uppington: It was about my cat.

Reporter: Ah yes - hello, little kitty, aren't you just *glassy*?

Our reporter left the interview and purchased a jam jar shaped like a cat from Mavis's jam stall and is now sitting in the corner stroking it and insisting it is called Arabella Clawington.

Home!

'Lucy!' Tiga cried, racing towards the little witch, who was standing by the front door like a kid waiting to be collected from school, rocking on her heels.

Fran lolloped along behind.

'You got Fran!' Lucy cheered. 'YOU ARE TIG-AMAZING!'

'I'm *Fabulous* Fran,' Fran corrected her with a tut. 'Or Franamazing.'

'You'll get used to her,' Tiga whispered to Lucy.

'Is it time to go home yet?' Lucy asked. 'I want to look for my backpack. It's got my entire Witch Wars collection in it – signed shrivelled heads and everything.'

'This isn't the way out …' Tiga mumbled, walking back through the doorway for the third time. 'But I'm sure it's the way we came in.'

Lucy nodded. 'It's definitely the same door.'

Tiga looked at the sign above it. ENTRANCE C. They had definitely come in via Entrance C, only now Entrance C no longer opened on to the path with the gate that led to the bridge. It led to somewhere completely different.

'Ooh!' Fran said, skipping out into the lavish garden.

Tiga couldn't believe it – a jelly-walled garden filled with hanging vines and floating roses, and the occasional jelly statue stretched out in front of them. She looked up into the trees. She could hear birds, but strangely, there didn't seem to be any in sight.

'Can you hear birds?' Lucy asked.

Fran cupped her hand to her ear. 'I can only hear my own fabulousness wafting from my being, I'm afraid.'

'Like I said,' Tiga said quietly to Lucy. 'You *will* get used to her.'

Fran skipped around the garden, scrunching up her

face every so often when she spotted a grotesque jelly statue. 'Come on! This way!'

'I suppose it must be this way,' Tiga said, trying to reassure herself.

'Ooh, ponies!' Fran cried as Tiga and Lucy rounded a perfectly pruned jelly hedge. There, standing tall in stables made of glossy black jelly, were two white jelly horses.

Tiga moved closer to read the signs. 'Cassidy and Sam. Jelly horses with names. Normal ...'

Lucy Tatty began leaping from foot to foot. 'Can we ride them? Pleeeease?!'

A Karen popped up from inside the stables. 'Absolutely not, darling. No riding the jelly horses. They are very fragile, darlings.'

Tiga tried to remember this Karen. She'd been one of the ones near the back in the tower.

'Did you get the jelly horses with someone's wish?' Fran asked.

Jelly-Horse Karen nodded as the horse prodded Fran with its muzzle.

'We're just trying to find our way out of here,' Tiga explained. 'How do we get back to the jelly bridge?'

Jelly-Horse Karen smiled. 'You'll have to pass the tests to get out of here now, darling.'

'The what?' Tiga asked in an almost-growl. She was getting tired of the Karens and their jelly.

'The tests. The twist of your wish, darling.'

'What *twist*?' Tiga pressed.

The Karen leaned over the stable door and snatched the piece of paper in Tiga's hand. She pointed at some tiny words. 'The twist.'

Tiga squinted at the paper and tried to focus – the words were smaller than any she'd ever seen before. They were even smaller than the words in Fran's favourite book: *Fabulous. Flawless. Fran.*

'I can't read *that*!' Tiga cried.

'Oh, very well, darling,' Jelly-Horse Karen said, holding it up to one eye which darted from left to right at rapid speed, like an enthusiastic spider in a pinball machine.

'Each wish will have a twist.'

'Did your wish have a twist?' Tiga asked Fran, but she just shrugged.

Jelly-Horse Karen coughed.

'And what is my twist?' Tiga said through gritted teeth.

'You have to complete three impossible tests to escape, darling.'

'And what if we don't pass the tests?' Lucy Tatty dared to ask.

'Oh, well then, darlings, you're stuck here … *FOR EVER*. Well, not for ever, darlings.'

'OH, THANK GOODNESS IT'S NOT FOR EVER!' Fran cried.

'No, darlings, just until you die.'

FLAWLESS FAIRY
ZARKLE
LAUNCHES A 'HOW TO BE
PERFECT' GUIDEBOOK

The flawless fairy Zarkle has launched a guide offering advice on how to be perfect. *Nonsensity* by Zarkle C. Sparkle is available from the Silver Stacks bookshop and includes tips such as:

NEVER STOP SMILING, EVEN WHEN SLEEPING.

And various other impossible things.

31

The Ghosts of the Fairy Caravan Park

'We're going to be stuck here until we *die*,' Fran said as Tiga marched on ahead, her fists clenched. The Karens could add all the twists they wanted; she was going to find that jelly bridge and get back to Silver City.

Up ahead was a gigantic jelly hedge surrounded by towers and spindly turrets. In the jelly hedge sat an ornate iron door with CHALLENGE ONE: FAIRY FLOP! carved on it. Tiga looked back. There was nothing but the wobbling main castle, and Fran, who was crying and wiping her tears away with Lucy Tatty's hair.

'Come on, hurry up! Let's get this over with,' Tiga said, as she pushed the door open.

The three of them walked reluctantly into the darkness. The door slammed shut behind them. All around smog swirled, and Tiga couldn't shake the sensation that at any moment she was going to fall down a deep, dark hole.

'Do you see that up ahead?' Lucy whispered.

Tiga squinted. She could just make it out. It looked like tiny red lights bobbing about in the distance, getting further and further away.

'WAIT!' Tiga cried, chasing after it.

'WAAAAAIT! WAAAAAAIT! WAAAAAIT!' her voice echoed in the eerie expanse.

'Wait, Tiga!' Lucy begged, running after her.

'Waaait, Tiiiiga. Waaait, Tiiiiiga. Waaait, Tiiiiga.'

'I'm just going to sit here,' Fran said, plonking herself down and tucking her knees under her chin. 'Has there been anyone more fabulous eeeever …'

Tiga squashed any thoughts of falling down black holes into a corner in her mind and pressed on through the darkness. She got closer and closer to the thing, her breath forming tiny desperate clumps of exhaustion in the frosty air. She stopped and rubbed her eyes. It couldn't be, could it?

'Are you seeing what I'm seeing?' Lucy Tatty panted.

Tiga rubbed her eyes again. There it was, a tiny ramshackle cart covered in red lights. In the middle of the cart, suspended from the arch of lights, was a lopsided lollipop with a badly painted face.

'Oh, hello,' the lollipop said. 'You're a long way from home. Are you ready for your first challenge?'

Tiga gasped and knelt down next to it.

'A pleasure to converse with you all,' the lollipop said grandly, its painted mouth moving, making the old paint flake and fall to the ground.

The squeaking sound it made when it spoke sounded like an old piece of metal trying to get out of bed.

'WHAT IS IT?!' Lucy Tatty screamed.

'WHAT ARE YOU?!' the lollipop screamed back. 'Only joking. You're a witch, I know that.'

'So you're a lollipop creature and a sort-of cart?' Tiga said nervously.

'Preposterous!' the thing said. 'I'm neither lollipop

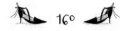

nor cart.' He lowered his voice to a whisper. 'I'm very glad to meet you. I almost never get visitors – it's very lonely here, and dark.'

Tiga awkwardly stroked the lollipop's cheek.

'I'm Moo,' he added, the lights on his cart flashing.

'Moo?' Tiga said.

Lucy giggled and slumped on the floor, clearly relieved the lollipop with the cart didn't seem to want to eat them.

Fran was silent in the distance, squinting at it with disdain, most likely because, given its bright lights, it looked a lot more 'show business' than she did.

'And you are?' Moo asked Fran.

'I'm FABULOUS,' she called over, throwing her head back dramatically.

'She's Fran, that's Lucy, and I'm Tiga,' Tiga said, glancing around, their surroundings now partially revealed by the bright red lights of Moo's cart.

Tiny caravans hung from branches like baubles on a Christmas tree, just like the fairy caravan park near Brollywood.

Moo turned with a creak and the lights on the cart glowed brighter, illuminating more of the caravan park. It stretched into the distance as far as Tiga could see.

'What is this, Moo?' she asked.

'It's a new addition,' Moo said. 'Just for you.'

'I don't like the sound of that,' Tiga groaned.

'WHO'S IN THOSE CARAVANS!' Fran bellowed, but there was only a ghostly silence and a squeak from the caravan swinging on a branch next to Tiga's head. She looked at Lucy Tatty and then tapped with a single finger on the door.

A fairy's head poked out of the window. But it wasn't a normal fairy head. Tiga could see right through it!

She screamed!

'Ghosts,' Lucy Tatty gasped.

'Actually, I prefer "expired fairy", thank you very much,' the ghost said, fluffing her matted hair.

Lucy Tatty wobbled and fainted, landing with an almighty thud.

Fran pointed at her.

'SUPERFAN DOWN.'

33

The Fairy Flop

'So you're dead?' Tiga asked, subtly nudging Lucy Tatty with her foot.

'So dead,' the expired fairy boasted.

'I miss being a fairy …' Fran said wistfully as the thing floated out of her caravan.

Lucy Tatty was beginning to come to. Tiga propped her up and watched as all around them, ghostly fairies began to swarm. Three assembled in front of them.

One, the expired fairy they had just been talking to, looked a lot like Crispy. The other looked like Donna, who Tiga remembered had refused to fly during the Witch Wars competition in order to make a point. And the third looked a lot like a mushroom in a dress.

'Moo,' the third one said. 'You aren't allowed to help them, you know.'

The lollipop swayed. 'I am aware, thank you.'

'Now,' the fairy who looked a lot like a dead Crispy snapped. 'We are your first test. We have been designed by the Karens and we are IMPOSSIBLE TO BEAT. We call this test The Fairy Flop.'

'Why flop?' Tiga asked.

'Like fairy, it also begins with F,' the fairy that looked like a mushroom said.

They floated closer.

'Now, remember, you can wish you knew the answer at any point. It just takes one wish to get out of this impossible challenge. Each of us has a special place in Sinkville history. We each belonged to a Top Witch. But which one belonged to Melissa Mushroomery?'

Tiga pointed at the fairy who looked like a mushroom. 'Her.'

The fairies stared blankly at Tiga. 'How did she know?' the one that looked like a mushroom whispered in awe.

'Golly, well done, Tiga,' Moo said, rattling his cart.

Fran high-fived Tiga.

'Fran,' Tiga said, looking from her hand to Fran's. 'Is your hand bigger?'

'Nah,' Fran said, holding up a giant-sized hand.

Tiga turned to the fairies. 'Now can we please leave?'

The fairies giggled. 'Yes. Say goodbye to Moo.'

'Goodbye, Tiga,' Moo said, sounding crushed. 'It was nice to meet you.'

'Wait!' Tiga cried. 'Why do I have to say goodbye to Moo?'

'This is where I live, in the Expired Fairy Caravan Park in the Jelly Castle Garden. Perhaps we will meet again one day.'

One of the fairies weaved closer. 'You know, you could *wish* that Moo could come with you.'

Tiga looked desperately at Fran, who was crying.

'NOT MOO!' she wailed.

'I didn't think she really liked Moo ...' Lucy Tatty mumbled.

Tiga bent down and hugged the little cart. 'I'll get

you out of here one day.' She turned to the fairies. 'And don't think I'll be making another wish in a hurry. I know about the twists, remember!'

'*Fine*,' the fairies said as one. Moo's face spun and smiled, and with a bang, Tiga, Fran and Lucy landed with a squidge back in front of the giant jelly hedge. This time the iron door was different, and the hedge was higher. The words had changed. Tiga got to her feet and moved closer to read what it said.

CHALLENGE TWO: CARAVAN CONUNDRUM.

33

Cloaks Galore

Senior Karen danced around in her gigantic new wardrobe filled with sparkly cloaks, singing 'Fran, Fran, For Ever'.

'Has there been anyone
More fabulous ever?
Nopedy nope!
Fran, Fran, for ever,
Darling.'

'Really sticks in your head, that song, doesn't it, darling?'

Senior Karen stopped and swiftly turned on her heel to face the witch who had dared to interrupt her. 'Oh, it's you. What is it, Karen?' she spat.

'Well, darling,' began Mismatched-Ears Karen.

'They passed the first test. The ghost fairies, Melissa Mushroomery, darling.'

'I told you to make the tests IMPOSSIBLE, DARLING!' Senior Karen roared.

Mismatched-Ears Karen nodded. 'It was, it really was!'

Senior Karen threw on a cloak and admired herself in the mirror as Karen the cat weaved between her legs. 'Well, make sure they can't pass the next one.'

'Yes, your darlingness. We are going to do another test with the fairies, only *much more difficult*.'

'Not difficult,' Senior Karen snapped. 'IMPOS-SIBLE. We want them stuck. We want them desperate enough to make many wishes!'

Mismatched-Ears Karen bowed her head and began backing towards the door. 'There's something else, darling. Probably nothing,' she added quietly.

'Well … SPEAK UP, darling, what is it?'

Mismatched-Ears Karen picked at her nails and whispered, 'Two more witches just arrived – on the Sinkville Express.'

'Wishers, darling?' Senior Karen asked eagerly.

Mismatched-Ears Karen shook her head. 'I think they're here to save Tiga … Lots of talk about Tiga.'

Senior Karen erupted into a fit of croaky cackles. 'Well, make sure they're stuck with Tiga and her little friends – more witches, more chance of wishes.'

34

Peggy and Felicity Fall into the Badlands

Tiga couldn't believe it when she saw Peggy and Felicity Bat somersaulting through the air and crash-landing in Fran's large beehive, which she was sure looked a lot more voluptuous than normal …

Felicity Bat levitated around Fran, trying to untangle Peggy, who was flailing and spluttering, 'Beehive! Trapped! Air!'

'What are you both doing here?!' Tiga cried. She'd never been so relieved to see Peggy, even if Fran's beehive had nearly suffocated her.

'We found some documents that suggested the Karens are dangerous and then we realised you were probably here. The Karens are extremely dangerous!' Peggy rambled. 'Their wishes have twists.'

'I know,' Tiga said glumly. 'I know …'

'If you see their jelly castle or their book, they can contact you, tempt you to make a wish,' Peggy explained. 'We need to get you out of here. Also, I really need to speak to Mavis about selling fake cats that are actually jam jars shaped like cats.'

'I should've known the Karens were trouble,' Tiga said, opening the Karens' book. Inside there was a new chapter, including a drawing of her screaming at the expired fairies.

'Tell them about Moo!' Lucy Tatty said, pulling on Tiga's sleeve.

Felicity Bat raised her hands in the air and flicked both fingers at once, finally freeing Peggy from the beehive and sending her head first into the iron door. Tiga helped her to her feet.

'It's gone!' Lucy Tatty gasped, as Tiga turned to see a very different-looking Fran. Whatever spell Felicity Bat had done to free Peggy had left nothing but a glittering bald head.

'What's gone?' Fran asked.

'The … time!' Tiga said quickly. 'Yes, where has the time gone? We've all known each other for so long now!'

Lucy Tatty pointed a finger at Fran's bald head. 'No, I meant her –'

'ON TO THE NEXT CHALLENGE!' Tiga roared, hoping Lucy would take the hint. She widened her eyes at Felicity Bat, who nodded and, with a quick flick, summoned a jelly hedge from the garden and placed it on Fran's head.

'What was that?' Fran asked, feeling her new hair.

Tiga held her breath.

'It's a jelly hedge!' Lucy Tatty said.

'No, dear,' Fran said, turning to Tiga and giving her a *where did you find this one* look. 'It's *hair*. Not h-e-d-g-e. Hair.'

'Hair?' Lucy Tatty said.

Fran patted her on the back. 'There you go! They say you learn a new thing every day.'

Lucy Tatty just stared at her.

'Righto,' Fran said chirpily, her hedge of hair wobbling. 'Onwards! Now we have more witches to help us get out of here.'

'Why?' Peggy asked. 'Are you lost?'

'No, dear, trapped,' Fran explained.

Tiga hung her head in shame. 'I made a wish … to get Fran out of here, but then they trapped me.'

Felicity Bat nodded. 'The twist, of course. They always add a twist to their wishes.' She tried to levitate up and out but something in the air forced her back down. She battled against it, pushing at the air above

174

her, a furious look fixed on her face. It was no good. She landed with a plop, like someone had switched her magic off.

'Ugh! *Great*, I'm stuck with three substandard witches and an oversized fairy with a hedge on her head,' she moaned.

'Oh, not you too,' Fran said. 'It's hair. H-a-i-r.'

Tiga wasn't paying attention. She was already heading for the door.

'What do you think that is?' Peggy said, as the door swung open to reveal hundreds of light bulbs, like a theatre show was beckoning them inside.

'SHOW BUSINESS,' Fran said, as if she was in a trance.

'SECOND CHALLENGE, DARLINGS,' a voice boomed, as all five of them were sucked into the doorway.

35

Caravan Conundrum

'GAME SHOW TIME!' the little fairy who looked like a mushroom in a dress said, cracking her knuckles.

'*Excuse* me,' Fran said, taking a large step forward. 'I present all Sinkville game shows.'

Tiga turned to see a large audience of expired fairies seated behind her. Most of the room was made of jelly, with a jelly stage and a jelly curtain. Bright lights flashed overhead, spelling out 'CARAVAN CONUNDRUM!'

Felicity Bat sighed. 'Seriously, Tiga. Why does stuff like this *always* happen to you?'

Peggy eyed the fairies suspiciously. 'Are they *dead*? Why can I see right through them?'

'They call themselves expired fairies,' Lucy Tatty whispered. 'They make me faint.'

'Remember, you can make a wish to get out of here at any time. Or wish to know the answer. Or wish for … a pony with your face painted on its hooves. *Anything.*'

'Yes,' Tiga said through gritted teeth. 'We *know.*'

'So, what's Caravan Conundrum?' Peggy asked, as five caravans on strings were winched down from the ceiling to her eye level.

'In one of the fairy caravans,' the fairy said grandly, 'I have hidden an extremely large and heavy rock. Tiga needs to figure out which caravan it is hidden in, *without* touching the caravans at all.' She folded her arms and smiled smugly. 'You can begin.'

One of the caravans strained and snapped from its string, landing with an almighty clang at Tiga's feet.

'That one,' Tiga said.

The fairy smacked her invisible head with her invisible hand. '*How* does she do it?!'

36

Put the Cauldron
Away, Karen

Senior Karen glided into the room where the other Karens were huddled.

'Darling, for the final test, I think we should do away with the expired fairies. What about a gigantic bat wearing *socks*?' Mismatched-Ears Karen suggested.

'Why socks, darling?' Tall Karen asked.

'Well, darling, it's strange, isn't it? Strange things are scary, darling.'

'Some strange things are just STUPID,' Small Karen said.

'WHY ARE THEY PASSING THE IMPOSSIBLE TESTS?!' Senior Karen screeched, making them all gasp.

'We didn't see you there!' Cheese-Grater Karen rambled nervously.

'Brains,' Tall Karen said. 'That's why they keep passing the tests. It's extraordinary.'

'SILENCE!' Senior Karen bellowed. 'The tests are stupid – the expired fairies, the caravans, that nonsense smog machine!' She stomped a foot on the smog machine, crushing it completely.

Smog-Machine Karen let out a faint wail.

'They must not complete the third challenge. We must keep them here for as long as possible,' Senior Karen went on. 'Let me deal with the third challenge.'

'Bravo, darling!' Trifle Karen said, stirring a cauldron.

'Why are you stirring a *cauldron*?' Senior Karen snapped. 'What's in it?'

'It's, well, nothing. Just bubbling water, darling, I thought it would look good – all witchy and so on.'

'PUT IT AWAY, DARLING,' Senior Karen demanded. 'You know the rules about boiling water.'

37

Cheats

With yet another bang, Tiga, Fran with her hedge hair, Lucy Tatty, Peggy and Felicity Bat landed with a thud back in the garden.

'We're right back where we started, again!' Fran cried. 'CHEATS!'

Tiga looked up to see a familiar sparkly cloak billowing in the wind.

'Congratulations on getting this far,' Senior Karen said, through gritted teeth. She was standing on a wobbling jelly balcony just above them, her face as angular as the mountain terrain that towered in the distance.

She turned and stared at Felicity Bat. 'Would you like to make a wish, darling?'

'Don't,' Tiga hissed.

'No,' Felicity Bat said, sounding like she was bored.

'You, darling?' Senior Karen said, pointing at Peggy.

Peggy linked arms with Tiga. 'NEVER.'

'Very well, worth a try,' she said, cracking a smile. 'Now for the final challenge. If you pass the test, you will be left at the jelly bridge. If not, you're stuck here.'

A measly puff of smog erupted next to Tiga. It was barely a puff at all.

'It's well and truly broken, darling,' Smog-Machine Karen said, emerging from behind a jelly wall and plonking the machine on the ground in front of Tiga.

Felicity Bat crossed her arms. 'What's this final test, then?'

Senior Karen cackled and croaked and then had a bit of a coughing fit. She cleared her throat and pointed at the new ornate iron door in the hedge. 'WARDROBE WARS!'

Felicity Bat put her head in her hands. 'Is nothing truly evil any more?'

38

Fran's Face

Back in Ritzy City, the pipe above Linden House began to groan and bulge until it burst, sending an aggressive waterfall down on the place.

Crispy hovered outside, muttering bad words under her breath as she watched her fabulous painting of Fran's face run down the wall.

'You know, I think it still looks like her,' Fluffanora said, taking a couple of steps back and nodding. 'It's more like Fran in the morning than Fran in the afternoon.'

The paint from the nose dribbled down into Fran's perfectly painted mouth.

'I'll just have to start again,' Crispy wailed, throwing her spindly arms in the air and flying towards Brew's fashion boutique.

'No!' Aggie Hoof cried. 'YOU CAN'T DEFACE *BREW'S*! IT'S HEAVEN!'

'Go for it,' Fluffanora said, pushing Aggie Hoof down a side street. 'It smells of cheese anyway.'

39

Wardrobe Wars

Tiga landed in a place so cluttered she couldn't make out its walls. It was large and filled with rails of sparkly cloaks, piles of shoes, some old tights and hundreds of wide-brimmed hats.

'WARDROBE WARS!' boomed Senior Karen from somewhere Tiga couldn't place. 'YOU HAVE TO FIGHT OFF ALL THE ITEMS IN THE WARD-ROBE AND ESCAPE! THREE-TWO-ONE A-GO.'

Tiga looked around just in time to see an army of glittering cloaks flying towards her. She tried to bat them away as a pair of sequinned leggings trotted over and tripped her up. A bunch of shoes landed on her and started lightly smacking her face while the cloaks hovered above her head.

'HELP!' Tiga cried. 'I'M BEING –' She didn't even want to say it, it was so silly. 'BEING ATTACKED BY RANDOM ITEMS OF CLOTHING! HELP!'

Four hats lined up and started rolling her faster and faster around the wardrobe.

'PEGGY?!' she cried. 'LUCY?! FELICITY?! … FRAN?'

'COMPLETE THE CHALLENGE TO BE RE-UNITED WITH YOUR FRIENDS,' Senior Karen's voice bellowed. 'OR MAKE A WISH TO ESCAPE.'

Tiga rolled back on to her stomach and started crawling fast towards the opposite corner, as the leggings trotted along behind her, kicking her every so often.

'MAKE IT STOP, KARENS!' she bellowed.

'ALL YOU HAVE TO DO,' came Senior Karen's booming voice, 'IS MAKE A WISH.'

'NEVER!' Tiga cried as she felt something wiggle in her pocket.

'DENNIS!' Tiga cried. 'I FORGOT ABOUT YOU!' She pulled the tights from her pocket and untied them

as two sparkly robes tried to scoop her up.

Dennis stretched his legs and bounded over to some questionable silver jumpsuits.

'Help me and I won't turn you in to Peggy,' Tiga pleaded.

Dennis hopped slightly on one foot, clearly contemplating the offer. Tiga grabbed a shoe that was kicking her in the chin and threw it at the cloaks.

'IT'S NOW OR NEVER, DENNIS!' Tiga roared, and just like that, Dennis sprang into action, stretching all the way around the wardrobe and scooping the cloaks and leggings, hats and kicking shoes into one neat pile.

Tiga felt around the walls. There didn't seem to be a door. She thought.

'YOU CAN STILL MAKE A WISH TO GET YOU OUT OF THERE,' came Senior Karen's voice.

'NO!' Tiga yelled, shouting up at nothing. Well, not nothing.

'A trapdoor, Dennis!' she cried.

Dennis made quick work of the bewitched clothes,

tying them into a fabulous knot with the spare pair of tights.

'Right, Dennis, now get me out of here!'

Dennis came bounding over and reached a leg up, knocking the door open and securing his foot on something. The other foot was on tiptoe, shaking next to Tiga.

'You can do it, Dennis,' Tiga said, as in one swift move Dennis lifted the foot in the air, wrapped it tightly around Tiga's waist and hoisted her up.

Um ...

'Darling, why are there some tights wrapped around my leg?' Smog-Machine Karen asked.

'Because that's where you put tights, darling,' Tall Karen said.

'No, no, darling,' said Smog-Machine Karen. 'These are not *my* tights, but they came out of that trapdoor and wrapped around my leg.

'Aren't they the criminal tights, darling?' Trifle Karen said to Jewel-Covered Karen.

Tiga was slowly hoisted into the room.

She gasped.

The Karens gasped.

'Strange way to make an entrance,' Small Karen squeaked.

'Ahha,' Tiga said, as Dennis unwrapped himself from her waist and tucked himself into Tiga's pocket. 'I win.'

'How *does* she do it?' Cheese-Grater Karen mused. 'You're as magical as a cheese grater.'

☆⟡☆

High up in one of the Jelly Castle turrets, Senior Karen bounced her head off a jelly desk, muttering, 'How. Did. She. Do. It?'

'Croak,' Karen the cat said.

Senior Karen swivelled to face the cat. 'I bet you a jelly tower that Tiga will destroy or hide our book, and her little friend Peggy will warn about taking the train to the Badlands. They'll block off all our contact like those meddling witches did years ago. How are we going to reach potential wishers now? We're never going to be able to get anything we want EVER AGAIN.' She planted her face in the jelly desk again.

'Perhaps you'd like to see this new cake from the new cake tower, darling, to cheer you up? We're calling them

Kakes,' Jelly-Horse Karen said, pushing an elaborate cream lump covered in swirls of black oozy stuff in front of her. 'It's a prototype, so it's not actually edible.'

Slowly, Senior Karen raised her head and looked at it, a glint of mischief in her eye. 'Karen, darling, you have just handed me the perfect plan ...'

'What kind of plan?' Jelly-Horse Karen asked.

'A cake plan, darling,' Senior Karen said with a croaky cackle. 'We're going to get one step ahead of them and transfer the power from the book to this cake. We'll give it to that kind little witch Peggy – ask her to put it in the baker's window. Say we need her to advertise our new business, darling. KAKES BY KARENS. We'll tell her we've turned good. We're not obsessed with wishes any more, we're obsessed with BAKING. She's too sweet not to believe it. Oh, darling, darling, *thousands* of witches must walk past the Ritzy City bakery every day, darling. They'll see our Kake, and soon we'll tempt all of Sinkville here!'

41

Free to Go, and Kake

'Well, that was all extremely weird,' Tiga said, as she stepped out of Entrance C, this time to find the jelly bridge there, along with her friends and a still-large Fran.

Tiga was sure Fran was even taller than before …

'Um, darling,' Jelly-Horse Karen said quietly to Peggy. 'We've stopped being strange and don't care about getting wishes any more.'

Peggy looked from the witch to the Jelly Castle. 'Well, that's excellent!'

Jelly-Horse Karen pulled her to the side and held out the weird prototype Kake. 'We're bakers now, darling. We were wondering if you would give it to the Ritzy City baker – if they put it in their window, it might drum up interest in our Kakes. Then we could send them lots of yummy wishes – I mean *Kakes*. It would really help us launch our business, darling.'

Peggy took the box and peered down at the Kake. She studied it for a moment before closing the box. 'This is a great idea,' Peggy said, beaming. 'Of course I will help you. You've made the right choice.'

Jelly-Horse Karen stared blankly at Peggy. 'So … you're taking the Kake?'

'Of course,' Peggy said kindly.

'Would you rather only eat a tub of Flappy Flora's Floral Foot Cream *for ever* or eat cheese water once?' Lucy Tatty asked, as she skipped around Peggy.

Tiga joined them and patted the cake box. 'What's this?'

'Just something for Cakes, Pies and That's About It Really,' Peggy said, as Felicity Bat shouted over to them.

'CAN WE *PLEASE* LEAVE NOW?'

Up high in the tallest jelly tower, Senior Karen watched eagerly as the little witches made their way

across the wobbling jelly bridge and off into the distance, the Kake box firmly tucked under Peggy's arm.

The entire journey home was a mash-up of Felicity Bat making fun of Tiga for always getting them into these messes, Tiga trying to change the subject, and Fran singing 'Fran, Fran, For Ever'.

They caught the Sinkville Express from the deserted Badlands station, which was made of jelly and peppered with signs saying WISHES THIS WAY.

'Well, at least everything can go back to normal now,' Peggy said with a sigh as the train trundled into the Ritzy City station.

'We should destroy this,' Tiga said, holding up the book. 'So no one finds it.'

'Agreed,' Peggy said. She nodded at Felicity Bat.

Felicity Bat wiggled. 'ACHOO!' she screamed in the direction of the book.

It promptly wilted and vanished.

'What?' Felicity Bat said, staring at their amazed

faces. 'The achoo spell is *easy* – even someone from above the pipes could do it.'

Tiga smiled. 'We're the only ones who have seen the Karens' book, and now it's gone. The Karens won't be able to lure any more witches to the Jelly Castle to do any more of their weird twist wishes.'

'What about Fluffanora?' Felicity Bat said. 'She's seen it.'

'Fluffanora would never trek all the way here to get something. And anyway,' Tiga said, 'she has pretty much everything she wants.'

Tiga smiled at the thought of seeing Fluffanora. She could feel Dennis wriggling about in her pocket.

'Wait,' she said. 'Why didn't Fluffanora come with you?'

Felicity Bat shrugged. 'We forgot to mention it.'

Tiga winced. 'She's not going to like that …'

Fluffanora is Offended

Fluffanora sat on the Linden House sofa, her hands neatly clasped in her lap.

'I can't *believe* you went to a weird jelly castle and nearly got trapped for ever without me. Let the record show, I am OFFENDED.'

Tiga laughed, relieved to be reunited with her friend.

'It's not funny, Tiga!' Fluffanora said, throwing a cushion at her. 'I'm glad you're safe, though. I can't believe the Karens are real.'

'They have changed their ways and are making cakes now. Kakes by Karen,' Peggy explained.

'I would *love* to see one,' Fluffanora joked.

'Well, you can,' Peggy said. 'There's one in the

window of Cakes, Pies and That's About It Really. I'm not sure if you'll be able to see it though. There's a giant cake shaped like Zarkle taking up almost all the space in the window display.'

'And where's witch-sized Fran? Is she back to her normal size yet?'

'No,' Tiga said. 'She wanted to see what it was like to have her jelly hair done at a witch-sized hairdresser. Felicity Bat's going to do a shrink spell on her later.'

'Hmm,' Fluffanora said. 'And the book?'

'Felicity achooed it,' Peggy explained. 'And I've banned any witch from travelling over the Badlands on the train. Everyone must get off at Silver City.'

Fluffanora shifted in her seat. 'Wait a frog, what was the twist on Fran's wish, then?'

But no one was listening.

'It's so strange my gran said she didn't write the book,' Lucy Tatty said, trying to touch the lace edging on Fluffanora's dress.

'Wait,' Fluffanora said, brushing Lucy's hand away.

'Gloria Tatty said she didn't write it? And you don't think that's odd?'

'We've been trapped in a jelly castle, with actual jelly horses, talking to expired fairies and playing Caravan Conundrum,' Tiga said defensively. 'So I'd say, no, actually, it's a tiny odd thing in a universe of much odder things.'

'I wonder why they don't leave the jelly castle,' Felicity Bat muttered, more to herself than to the others. 'That would be a much easier way of enticing witches to make wishes … face to face.'

'Um, Tiga …' Fluffanora said.

'I think it's safe to say we made a mistake, but we've kept it under control!' Tiga said, lamely punching the air with her fist.

The chandelier shook. The ground rumbled.

'Tiga!' Fluffanora said, pointing out of the window. 'Is that Fran?'

A fairy almost as tall as the tallest Ritzy Avenue building stomped past just as a letter floated through the window and landed in Tiga's lap.

WISH YOUR FRIEND WOULD STOP GROWING
BEFORE SHE **BURSTS?**
WISH SHE WAS BACK TO HER NORMAL FAIRY
SIZE?

You saw our book - you know that
WE CAN MAKE YOUR WISHES COME TRUE
(not like a genie, we're better than
that rubbish).

VISIT THE KARENS! You'll find us in:
   The Jelly Castle,
   Boulder Boulevard,
   The Badlands,
   Sinkville.

Don't bring a hot bath, or else.

'Those monsters!' Tiga cried. 'That was the twist on
Fran's wish. She wished to get bigger, so she's going to
get bigger … until she bursts!'

ZARKLE MALFUNCTIONS

Gretal Green's latest invention, a perfect fairy made in under five minutes, shrivelled up this morning into a small, singed thing that looks not unlike an above-the-pipes fly.

Gretal Green believes the fairy malfunctioned due to excessive, constant smiling.

'I once saw her sleeping,' said Mavis of Jam (And Sometimes Cats) Stall 9. 'She was doing her mad, toothy smile and snoring at the same time. It was weird.'

Gretal Green said she did explain to Zarkle that she could take a break from smiling, but Zarkle didn't know what she was talking about.

It is not known whether Zarkle will continue to present *Cooking for Tiny People*, but Gretal Green is said to be trying to find a job better suited to Zarkle - something that fits with her love of teeth ...

In other news, Top Witch Peggy Pigwiggle has banned anyone from riding the Sinkville Express past Silver City into the Badlands, not that any witch would do that anyway. And a reminder that there is to be no riding in the carriage smeared with jam, because it falls off the tracks sometimes.

43

By the Fountain

Tiga leapt off the Sinkville Express and clattered down the steps.

'Tiga!' Gretal Green cried from where she was perched on the fountain.

Tiga raced over.

'Oh, Tiga, Peggy told me you'd gone to the Badlands. I sent the slugs to look for you – thank goodness you're all right.'

Tiga nestled under her mum's arm. The fountain drizzled behind them, the silver stilts of the city shining. There was nowhere in the world Tiga would've rather been. She sneakily dropped Dennis the tights out of her pocket and he scurried off through the fountain.

'What *is* that splashing?' Gretal Green said, turning to look.

'Lalalalala nothing!' Tiga shouted, awkwardly grabbing her mum and pulling her into a hug.

She told her mum all about the Karens, and about the spell they had put on Fran. The one that would end in her bursting.

Every so often, witches would stroll past, completely unaware of the mother and daughter sitting on the fountain, their hearts heavy, their brains scrambling for solutions.

'We'll find a way to save her, Tiga, I promise. It's the least I can do for causing so much trouble with Zarkle. She malfunctioned, anyway.'

Tiga heard the echo of Fran's voice from the first time she landed in Sinkville, on top of Mavis's jam stall.

NO BROKEN BONES OR DEATH! WELL DONE.

'She saved me,' Tiga said sadly. 'She's infuriating, and loud, and completely self-absorbed … and *glittery*, but without her –'

Tiga couldn't finish.

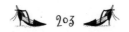

'I know,' Gretal Green said, hugging her tighter. 'We won't let her burst. You should tell her about it, though. It's only fair she knows what's happening to her. She'll get an awful fright if she keeps getting bigger.'

'How big do you think she'll grow?' Tiga asked, but not even Gretal Green could've predicted that.

44

Massive

Two Weeks Later ...

Tiga flicked her finger and poured herself a cup of Trilly's tea. She was alone in Linden House with Peggy. It was nice to have some time with her, just the two of them; she so rarely got to see her best friend now she was so important.

Tiga had mentioned the growing and bursting to Fran. She'd taken it surprisingly well, screaming for only ninety-seven hours.

'We destroyed the book, the Sinkville Express is under control, now all I have to do is figure out how to stop an oversized fairy from bursting and catch a pair of criminal tights.'

Tiga smiled. 'Being the Top Witch isn't easy ...

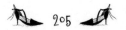 205

Wait, criminal tights? You're still after them? How far have you got?'

Fran knocked on the window; a huge fist covered in glitter was all they could see. Tiga poured an extra cup and placed it gently between her mammoth fingers.

'THANK YOU KINDLY, MY DEAREST TIGA!' Fran's voice bellowed, making everything shake.

'This is out of control,' Peggy whispered, steadying a lamp that looked ready to topple off the table.

'I'M GOING FOR A QUICK DIP BY THE COVES, DEARS!'

Witches screamed as Fran bounded off down the road, crushing a couple of lamp posts as she went.

'We need to fix this,' Peggy said, joining Tiga at the window.

'OOPS, SORRY, PARDON ME,' Fran apologised, as witches scattered to avoid her gargantuan sparkly shoes.

Julie Jumbo Wings flew past her. 'Ha! Who's got the JUMBO WINGS now!'

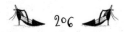

Fran swatted her away, sending her straight down someone's chimney.

'I'm glad Fran's given up trying to fly,' Peggy said. 'That's at least something.'

Tiga thought back to the day before, when Fran had tried to fly and got the Pearl Peak mountain stuck up her nose. She gripped the window frame tighter and watched her fairy friend skip off into the distance. 'There must be *something* to make her small again. There's got to be something …'

No One Can See the Kake

Meanwhile, back in the Jelly Castle …

'THAT PEGGY PIGWIGGLE DIDN'T PUT OUR KAKE IN THE WINDOW OF THE BAKER'S OR IF SHE DID SOMETHING IS WRONG BECAUSE THE WITCHES OF RITZY CITY CLEARLY CAN'T SEE IT, DARLING. CAN THEY?'

'I wonder what it is,' Cheese-Grater Karen said cheerily.

'SILENCE!' Senior Karen roared. 'Only one witch has seen the Kake apart from Tiga and her friends, and that's the baker at Cakes, Pies and That's About It Really! Are you *sure* you're sending the wish slips to her at the right address, darling?'

Trifle Karen nodded frantically. 'Oh yes, I am. The Cakes, Pies and That's About It Really baker lives at The EXTREMELY Hot Oven in Cakes, Pies and That's About It Really, 87 Ritzy Avenue, Ritzy City, Sinkville.'

'THE BAKER IS CLEARLY NOT GETTING THE WISH SLIPS, DARLINGS!' Senior Karen said, her face turning fuchsia. 'AND NO ONE ELSE IN RITZY CITY HAS SEEN THE KAKE!'

'Well, I'm baffled,' Trifle Karen said. 'Baffled, darling.'

FRAN STILL HUMONGOUS. GREAT TROUBLE ON THE SET OF *COOKING FOR TINY PEOPLE*

Fran is still massive, and growing by the day. This has caused a number of problems for Sinkville, mainly that we seem to be existing in a permanent storm of glitter. There are fears Fran could combust at any moment.

Cooking for Tiny People has also suffered a blow. Fran, with her gigantic hands, is unable to use any of the kitchen equipment without crushing it. So far she has destroyed:

11 tiny ovens

8 tiny fridges

95,000 tiny spoons

Some witches think she should be replaced,

but no one has the guts to say it in case she glitters them. Our reporter interviewed Fran yesterday and made the suggestion.

Reporter: You should quit *Cooking for Tiny People*, I think.
Fran: EXCUUUUUSE ME?!
Reporter: I have glittery dust IN MY EYES.

End of interview.

A WARNING MESSAGE: it has been brought to our attention that our sister paper, the *Silver Times*, is running a campaign encouraging witches to return the SORRY-WE-THOUGHT-YOU-WERE-EVIL-AND-LEFT-DURING-THE-BIG-EXIT-WHEN-REALLY-YOU-WERE-JUST-SUCKED-INTO-A-HAT gift baskets from

Cakes, Pies and That's About It Really. A bunch of them with RETURN TO SENDER tags have been raining down on the city, knocking people over, shattering chimneys, breaking windows, splatting on statues and confusing cats. Please be careful.

Return to Sender

The gift basket came careering through the air. 'Whoa, look how fast that one's going!' a witch shouted as it hurtled through the window of Cakes, Pies and That's About It Really, shattering the glass and the giant cake shaped like Zarkle.

Witches crowded around the window.

'Will you look at that one,' a witch said, pointing like she was in a trance at the strange-looking cake. 'Kakes by Karen,' she said. 'Kakes by Karen.'

✫ ✫ ✫

Senior Karen skipped around the Jelly Castle, making it wobble uncontrollably.

The rest of the coven charged into her tower, keen to know what was going on.

'We've had an influx of potential witch wishers, darlings!' Senior Karen croaked with glee. 'Hundreds of them! Our Kake seems to be working again …'

Australia?

Felicity Bat arrived back at Linden House, closely followed by Fluffanora and Aggie Hoof, who were arguing about how big is too big for a hat.

'The size of a building,' Aggie Hoof said, 'is about as big as a hat should be.'

'Sometimes I wonder if you're real,' Fluffanora mused.

'I've got it, I've got it,' Felicity Bat said grandly, sweeping into the Linden House sitting room, a crinkled old map tucked up under her arm. '*Australia.*'

'Is that a spell to make Fran small again?' Peggy asked.

'No,' Felicity Bat said, unrolling the map. 'It is *Australia.*'

'Australia,' Tiga said, her head in her hands.

'It's a place and it has a lot of land, lots of large, unpopulated land. It would be safe to send Fran there,' Felicity Bat said. 'You know … so she doesn't burst on us.'

'Are you serious?' Peggy said.

'It's above the pipes and it's big,' Felicity Bat said with a nod.

Tiga scowled. 'We are *not* going to banish Fran above the pipes to Australia to burst!'

Felicity Bat levitated around the room, picking at her nails. 'Why not? We've tried everything. Shrink spells, potions, lotions, squash machines … There's nothing left to do.'

Peggy shot her a look.

'So you think we should just GIVE UP?!' Tiga cried, clenching her fists. Sometimes she *hated* Felicity Bat.

A gigantic hand reached in the window of Linden House and placed a pinky on Tiga's shoulder. **'If I must go, then I must go … to Austrapalina.'**

'Australia,' Tiga corrected her.

'Astrangalatopilanta,' Fran tried again.

'Australia,' Tiga said.

'Austraplatinapappa.'

'She can't even *say it*!' Tiga said, throwing her hands in the air.

Fran's humongous eye peered in at them.

'There must be something we're missing,' Tiga said desperately. She just couldn't understand. They had to be able to fix her somehow.

'Fine, I'll keep looking into it,' Felicity Bat said, levitating around the room. 'But you have to appreciate that even *I* might not be able to solve this one.'

Tiga picked up Lucinda Bunch's notebook and began to pace the room. 'Perhaps we've been looking at this all wrong. Everything we've done so far has been focused on trying to fix Fran. Maybe what we need to do is fix the Karens. Finish what Lucinda Bunch started all those years ago once and for all.'

Felicity Bat stroked her chin. 'You know what, Tiga? For once, you might be right.'

'Really? You think so?' Tiga asked, although she didn't want to believe it. She wanted Felicity Bat to shout, 'Nonsense! We don't ever need to go back to that jelly castle!' But Tiga knew that wouldn't happen, because there was only one really good reason none of their spells were working on Fran. The Karens were still going strong.

'Yes,' Felicity Bat said with a nod. 'You're right, the Karens are still going strong.'

'I didn't say that!' Tiga cried. 'She's mind reading again, Peggy!'

Peggy opened her mouth to say something, but Felicity Bat slipped a piece of paper in to stop her.

'Mhut mar mu moing?'

'They're on the lookout for more wishers again,' Felicity Bat explained as Tiga fished the piece of paper out of Peggy's mouth. 'Read it. I got it just before I walked in here.'

DO YOU WISH EVERYONE WOULD JUST BELIEVE THAT YOU ARE NO LONGER EVIL AND ANNOYING?

You saw our Kake - you know that
WE CAN MAKE YOUR WISHES COME TRUE
(not like a genie, we're better than
that rubbish).

VISIT THE KARENS! Take the Sinkville
Express to The Badlands and follow signs
for:
  The Jelly Castle,
  Boulder Boulevard - access via
  Entrance C.

Tiga stared up at Felicity Bat, who was levitating awkwardly above her. 'Felicity, I ...'

'Don't worry about it, Tiga!' Felicity Bat said, faking a cackle. 'That would *never* be my wish.'

'I don't think you're evil,' Tiga said. 'Honestly.'

'Nor do I!' Peggy added.

'NOR ME,' Fran bellowed.

'I'm on the fence,' Fluffanora joked.

Felicity Bat straightened her hat and cleared her

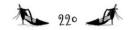

throat. 'Well. I hope I'm still a bit annoying. Genius can be infuriating to be around – all that perfect levitating and brilliant spells.'

'*Fine*,' Tiga said through gritted teeth. 'You're annoying. But we love you.'

Felicity Bat looked awkwardly at Tiga. Tiga stared back at Felicity Bat, a strange feeling swirling in her stomach. 'Wait a second,' she said. 'Something is weird.'

'It's my face,' Felicity Bat said apologetically. 'Happy emotions make it look bizarre.'

'No,' Tiga said slowly, scanning the wish paper from the Karens. Her eyes stopped dead on a sentence that was new.

You saw our Kake.

'Kake!' Tiga cried. 'THEY TRICKED US!'

'YES, CAKE! FETCH THE CAKE!' Fran roared. **'IN A CRISIS, ROLL OUT THE CAKE. THAT'S WHAT I SAY IN CHAPTER FOUR OF MY BOOK *FABULOUS. FLAWLESS. FRAN.*'**

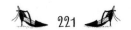

221

'No,' Tiga said, shaking her head. 'It usually says you've seen our book, meaning *The Karens*, which we destroyed. But now it says Kake.'

Peggy turned slowly to look at her, her face warping from cheery to crushed. 'The cake they gave me. The one I gave to Cakes, Pies and That's About It Really, to put in their window.'

'Ugh!' Tiga cried. 'Taking advantage of Peggy's kindness. What complete toads!'

'When I was levitating here, I noticed the Cakes, Pies and That's About It Really window was smashed – something about a gift basket flying through the window. I saw the Kake sitting there, prominently displayed,' Felicity Bat said, casually floating about the room. 'Should I smash the Kake?'

'Yes, please,' Peggy said. 'Squash it.'

Felicity Bat clapped her hands. 'Done,' she said smugly.

'Your powers worry me sometimes …' Peggy said.

'I'll show you how to do it. Hold your hands up and –'

There was a rumble of witches' feet. Excited screeches competed with the howling wind, a whiff of tragedy and sinister cake in the air.

Peggy walked slowly to the window, as tiny bits of paper swarmed angrily outside. 'This is all about to get *way* out of control,' she said, opening the window and catching one.

Nottie, Owner of Jam Stall 7,

DO YOU WISH YOU WERE THE ONLY STALL THAT SOLD CATS AND JAM? THEN VISIT THE KARENS!

You saw our Kake - you know that
WE CAN MAKE YOUR WISHES COME TRUE
(not like a genie, we're better than
that rubbish).

VISIT THE KARENS! Take the Sinkville Express to the Badlands and follow signs for:

```
The Jelly Castle,
Boulder Boulevard -
access via Entrance C.
```

```
No hot drinks, thank you.
```

'Oh, frogtruffles, hundreds of witches must've seen that Kake by now,' Peggy said quietly.

'They'll all race to the Badlands now,' Fluffanora added.

Peggy paced back and forth. 'I'll shut down the Sinkville Express.' She nodded at Felicity Bat, who flew obediently out of the door. 'That'll slow them down.'

Tiga got up and took the piece of paper flapping in Peggy's hand, as witches raced past the window waving little wish slips above their heads, squealing and occasionally banging into lamp posts and walls. 'This is a disaster …'

Peggy in Trouble

Peggy tried to calm the growing crowd of furious witches standing outside Linden House.

'OPEN UP THE SINKVILLE EXPRESS. WE WANT TO VISIT THE KARENS!'

'WE WANT TO GET WISHING!'

'THEY PROMISED ME RICHES!'

'THEY PROMISED ME NEW TOES.'

Peggy shook her head, her hands raised in the air, urging them to hush. 'The Karens are incredibly dangerous. I was recently trapped inside the walls of their jelly castle.'

The crowd fell silent.

'It was awful,' Peggy added, before everyone burst out laughing.

'HOW COULD A JELLY CASTLE BE AWFUL?' someone cried. 'IT'S ABSOLUTELY MAGICAL.'

'B-b-b-but,' Peggy stuttered. 'Look what they did to Fran.' She thrust her hand in Fran's direction. She was curled up in the street like a gigantic pooch. She waved and smiled, delighted with the attention.

'Look more distressed,' Tiga hissed at her, but Fran couldn't hear.

'SHE WANTED TO BE THAT SIZE, AND THAT'S WHAT SHE GOT!' someone shouted.

Tiga stepped forward, standing next to Peggy. 'No, Fran just wanted to be witch-sized, but the Karens tricked her.'

'SERVES HER RIGHT FOR NOT SPECIFYING WHAT SIZE SHE WANTED TO BE!' a witch yelled.

'EXCUSE YOU?' Fran bellowed, getting to her feet, the ground rumbling as she did so. She loomed large over the crowd, waggling a fist.

'WELL, IF YOU WON'T TELL FELICITY BAT TO REMOVE THE GIGANTIC SPIKY WALL AROUND THE STATION AND LET US ON THE

SINKVILLE EXPRESS, WE'LL JUST FLY TO THE BADLANDS!' a witch shouted.

'That'll take ages,' Fluffanora said casually.

Peggy bit her lip. 'We need to control this,' she whispered to Tiga before clapping her hands. 'VERY WELL. I WILL REOPEN THE SINKVILLE EXPRESS SO YOU CAN GET TO THE KARENS AS QUICKLY AS POSSIBLE. IT WILL JUST TAKE A BIT OF TIME TO GET IT BACK UP AND RUNNING.'

'What?' Tiga cried.

The witches in the crowd leapt up and down, shouting things like 'WISHES!' and 'JELLY BUILDINGS!'

Peggy turned to Tiga. 'I'll stall them as much as I can, but I won't be able to hold them for long. They'll fly otherwise. You have two hours to figure out how to stop the Karens once and for all.'

49

Fluffanora Knows the Answer

'YOU SEEM STRESSED, TIGA. MAY I OFFER YOU A MASSAGE?' Fran asked, reaching towards Tiga with a hand gigantic enough to crush the whole of Linden House.

'No!' Tiga said quickly, ducking to avoid it. 'Thank you, though.'

Fran took a seat, wedging herself between the buildings of Ritzy Avenue and sending the pavement rippling like a delighted wave.

Tiga paced back and forth; she tried to grab hold of her thoughts and steady them, but like a disobedient pony, they galloped on, making her brain feel as unsteady as her feet.

There was only one person who might be able to help her, one person who was just the right amount of weird and brains to fix this – her mum. But she was miles away in Silver City. The Sinkville Express was out of action and they couldn't start it up again without a bunch of witches jumping on and racing to the Karens' jelly castle. It would take three to five hours to fly to Silver City, depending on the wind, even if she persuaded Felicity Bat to levitate and give her a lift. She momentarily contemplated some sort of time-freeze spell, but even that could take hours of looking through the Linden House library.

Felicity Bat came gliding down the street. 'Any ideas? They're queuing up outside Ritzy City station, little pieces of paper in hand …'

Tiga shook her head. 'Zero ideas.'

'Here,' Fluffanora said, handing her a takeaway Clutterbucks. 'What are you thinking?'

Tiga sighed and explained she needed to get to her mum but there was no quick way, especially without the Sinkville Express.

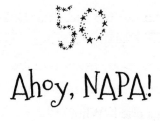

Ahoy, NAPA!

Gretal Green stood in her NAPA office in Silver City, fiddling with a string of teeth Zarkle had brought her.

'And I hope you paid the above-the-pipes children for these?' she said sternly. 'You didn't *steal* them?'

Zarkle, now shrivelled and fly-like, still had a perfect smile. She nodded and jiggled a coin purse. 'I always pay.'

There was a rumble, subtle at first, but soon strong enough to dislodge the books from their shelves, sending them tumbling to the ground.

'What the frogtruffles?' Gretal Green spluttered, the string of teeth wriggling in her hand.

BOOM.

BOOM.

BOOM.

Gretal Green walked to the window and squinted at the large thing that was bounding towards them as Zarkle disappeared with a pop.

'Oh, you're just going to leave me on my own?' Gretal Green said, as the thing gained ground, now close enough for her to make it out.

'Fran?' she said, as Tiga, perched precariously on the fairy's shoulder, came into view.

'MUM! IT'S ME!' she cried, waving madly.

'Tiga!' Gretal Green shouted, opening the window and holding out her arms. 'That looks incredibly dangerous!'

'I'M AS STRONG AS A FABULOUS, GLITTERY ROCK, DON'T YOU WORRY, GRETAL GREEN.'

Tiga clambered through the window, followed by Felicity Bat and Fluffanora.

'Hello, girls,' Gretal Green said, sounding slightly baffled. She frowned. 'Fran is even more massive, I see …'

'Mum,' Tiga said urgently, grabbing her mum's arm. 'We need help. The Karens. Two hours to stop them. Wishes. Everyone. Sinkville is going to be plunged into jelly-covered chaos.'

'Slow down, slow down,' Gretal Green said, giving Tiga a hug. 'What is going on?'

Tiga explained everything – the Kake, the wishes, the urgent need to stop the Karens.

Gretal Green nodded. 'I suspected perhaps the key to making Fran small again was to deal with the Karens. It seems like a somewhat unbreakable spell. I sent the spy slugs to the Badlands to do some detective work. I sent them at first to look for you, but by the time they got there you'd come back. I left them there to gather more information. I'm fascinated by that jelly castle. There's nothing like it anywhere else in Sinkville.'

'Is Sluggfrey there?' Tiga asked. She didn't like the idea of her slug being in the Badlands.

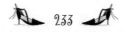

Gretal Green nodded. 'He's fine. He's very well trained. Now, let's start with slugs.'

Tiga looked at the window of her mum's office – it was lined with screens that showed each of the slugs' views.

Fran, exhausted from the run from Ritzy City, began to sway, her head lolling, her eyelids closing.

'Fran,' Tiga said slowly. 'FRAAAAN!' But it was too late – the fairy's enormous head went straight through the window, smashing the screens.

'Fran!' they all shouted at once.

'**SHOW BUSINESS!**' Fran snorted, snapping out of her slumber.

'What are we going to do now?' Tiga cried, picking up a shard of smashed screen.

'Not to worry,' her mum said. 'I can probably hook the slug view up to some spoons and we can watch it on those!'

It was one of the many things Tiga loved about her mum – she never gave up.

Tiga sat in her mum's desk chair and peered at all the spoons hovering in front of her. Her mum was clicking her fingers, trying to tune each of the TVs to the slugs' views.

Tiga could see the hazy darkness of the Badlands in all except one, which was showing a rerun of Fran on *Cooking for Tiny People* before she was gigantic. She was making a pineapple head.

Tiga felt a lump in her throat. Everything was beginning to feel completely hopeless. She'd saved Fran from the Karens, but that didn't seem to matter; soon Fran would be gone. She just couldn't win.

The image on the final spoon flicked from Fran to another slug view. This time in the Jelly Castle Garden.

'That's Sluggfrey,' Gretal Green said.

Tiga grabbed the spoon and held it tightly, as if by holding it as tightly as she could, the Karens couldn't get him.

'What *is* that?' Felicity Bat asked.

'Move forward,' Gretal Green ordered.

Sluggfrey obliged and stopped right next to something: a toad climbing on a jelly horse.

'I didn't see any toads when we were there, did you?' Felicity Bat said to Tiga.

'Well, toads are quite small, so you might not see them,' Fluffanora said.

'Turn right,' Tiga said.

There, in the corner of the garden, was another toad, only this time next to the broken smog machine.

'They used the smog machine to try to make the place creepy,' Tiga explained to Fluffanora.

'Two toads,' Felicity Bat said. 'Do you not think that's strange?'

But no one was listening to her.

'I don't think this is going to help,' Tiga said. 'I can't see a Karen in any of the spoons.'

Felicity picked up a spoon with an interior view of the jelly castle.

A toad waddled past.

A toad carrying a cheese grater.

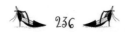

FRAN SMASHES MAVIS'S JAM STALL

'She just came crashing past and squashed the lot. Every time someone ruins my jam (and sometimes cat) stall! EVERY TIME,' Mavis told our reporter.

Unfortunately, our reporter fainted due to UTTER FEAR before finishing this interview. The fainting occurred because Mavis recently befriended Zarkle, the fairy who once presented *Cooking for Tiny People* but now collects teeth. Our reporter found out that Zarkle suggested Mavis could spruce up the cats she was selling at her jam (and sometimes cat) stall by giving them some teeth. Big teeth she'd collected from above-the-pipes children. 'Witches would like that,' Zarkle said.

They secured the teeth with jam.

'It's not terrifying,' Zarkle said.

51

Help?

'ALMOST READY!' Peggy cried from inside the Sinkville Express station. Outside, a beefy line of eager witches waited for the doors to open. She looked at her watch. Only thirty minutes to go …

'Tiga,' she whispered to herself. 'You had better think of something fast!'

Felicity Bat
Figures It Out

'They're toads,' Felicity Bat said, levitating around the room grandly, as she liked to do.

'What are you talking about?' Tiga said.

'Toads. The Karens are toads. I did wonder why they never left the jelly castle. Surely, if you wanted to ask a witch to make a wish, you'd just fly out of there and come to Ritzy City, but no. They sat there quietly for years, waiting for someone to discover the book, or for the Sinkville Express to start up again. And unfortunately for us, thanks to Tiga, both happened pretty much at the same time.'

'They can't be toads!' Tiga laughed. 'I saw them. You saw them. They were witches.'

'You know,' Gretal Green said, getting to her feet and

walking over to Felicity Bat, 'my spy slugs see past certain magic concoctions, anything that would prevent them from spying accurately. Things like spells to hide or disguise, that sort of thing.'

'So wait a minute,' Fluffanora said. 'There's a chance the Karens are coated in a spell that would make them look like witches when, say, Tiga sees them, but actually they're just toads?'

Tiga had to sit down. 'But *toads*?' she said. '*Really?*'

'Who do you think put the spell on them in the first place, then?' Fluffanora asked Felicity Bat.

She shrugged. 'Not sure, but I have my suspects.'

'Who?' Fluffanora asked eagerly, but she was interrupted by a gasp from Tiga.

'We only have twenty minutes left!'

'Twenty minutes?' Gretal Green asked.

Tiga nodded frantically. 'Yes. Peggy is trying to stop the town from going to the Karens by themselves. She told them she'd open the Sinkville Express if they were patient. It was a way of buying us some time to fix this, but she only gave us a couple of hours.'

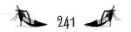

'She'll be panicking by now,' Felicity Bat said. 'I shouldn't have left her alone.'

Gretal Green paced the room. 'Well, let's look at what we've got so far. The Karens are toads, coated in some sort of spell that makes them appear to be witches. Spells like that always have something that keeps them going – Tiga, think of it like an above-the-pipes battery. Without the battery, the spell wears off.'

'And,' Tiga said, her eyes wide, 'if the spell wears off, the Karens would just be toads again!'

'Exactly,' Gretal Green said with a nod.

'So what is the thing, what's the battery?' Tiga asked.

Gretal Green scrunched up her nose and looked deep in thought. Fluffanora was holding a spoon looking at a slug view of the jelly castle, and Felicity Bat was looking at the little wish slip the Karens had sent her.

Felicity Bat levitated lower. 'They mention here not to bring a hot bath. Why would someone do that? Bring a hot bath to the Badlands?'

'**TO WASH,**' Fran suggested, making the office rattle.

'And,' Felicity Bat went on, 'on that wish slip we caught careering through the air for Nottie, it had something about hot drinks.'

'Very strange,' Gretal Green said.

'It's like they're afraid of them for some reason.'

Felicity Bat grinned. 'I know how to do it. How to break the spell.'

'BRAVO!' Fran cheered, patting Felicity Bat on the back and sending her somersaulting across the room, straight into a wall.

'If she's dead,' Fluffanora said, turning to Fran, 'you are definitely going to burst.'

'Hot water,' Felicity Bat said from the crumple of limbs and hat and shoes she had rolled into in the corner. 'They are scared of hot water, because –'

Fluffanora waved the spoon. 'Because it would melt this.'

Tiga picked it up and stared at it. 'The jelly castle. You're a genius, Felicity Bat!'

'Obviously.'

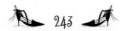

Tiga grinned. 'But how do we melt such an enormous jelly castle?'

Fluffanora put down her takeaway Clutterbucks cup in front of Tiga and sighed. 'It seems impossible.'

Tiga stared at the cup, her eyes wide. 'I HAVE AN IDEA!'

53

Gloria Explains

The plan was simple, and inspired by the pipe Gretal Green had rigged in Tiga's bedroom to transport Clutterbucks drinks direct from the Clutterbucks café. They'd do the same, only on a much bigger scale, and to a pipe directly above the jelly castle in the Badlands. All of them would hide in the Sinkville Express, with the hundreds of excited witches who wanted to make wishes. When they passed the pipe, Felicity Bat would levitate up and activate it, spilling gallons of hot Clutterbucks cocktails down on to the jelly castle, melting it and turning the Karens back into toads. Fran, meanwhile, would sneak along behind – but far enough back that the Karens wouldn't see her until the hot Clutterbucks was raining down on their castle. At first

Tiga was reluctant to bring Fran, but Felicity Bat persuaded her it was a good idea. As the well known saying goes, you never know when you might need a glittery giant.

The potential downside of the whole plan was the contraption failed to work and all the witches made wishes, wreaking havoc on Sinkville. Who knew how gigantic the Karens' castle would get if they granted all those new wishes? Tiga shuddered at the thought of such 'expansion, darling'.

Tiga marched past the Silver City fountain, the others scuttling along behind.

'Wait! Tiga!' came a familiar cry. 'YOUR NUMBER ONE FAN NEEDS YOU!'

'No time, Lucy!' Tiga said, turning to see her little friend racing towards her, a bandy-legged, high-kicking grandmother at her side.

'Oh, hello, Gloria Tatty,' Tiga said.

'GLORIA TATTY!' Fluffanora said, clutching her heart. 'I love *Melissa's Broken Broom*. Why did you say you didn't write *The Karens*, when clearly you did?'

Gloria Tatty looked taken aback. 'Because I didn't write it.'

'Well, it doesn't matter,' Felicity Bat said. 'We've figured out how to destroy the Karens and we're off to do that now. They've already got to most of the witches in Ritzy City, and it won't be long before they get to the witches of Silver City. I hope you're pleased with yourself.'

Gloria Tatty grabbed Tiga's arm. 'You must not destroy the Karens!'

'We have to,' Tiga said, twisting free of her grasp. 'And we're running out of time.' She made to walk away, but Gloria Tatty leg-kicked her way around so she was standing in front of her, blocking her path.

'Really, Gloria,' Gretal Green said, stepping in. 'What is all this about?'

Tiga stared at Gloria Tatty, trying to work her out. Every eye twitch, every wrinkle, every slight curling of the lip, none of it revealed anything about her. She definitely wasn't evil, but why would she want the Karens to keep going?

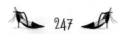

'Lucy told me you met Moo,' she said quietly.

'Moo?' Felicity Bat asked.

'My friend, Moo,' Gloria Tatty said sadly. 'My *only* friend, Moo.'

Tiga gasped. She remembered what Gloria Tatty had said all those weeks ago in Rainbow Bones.

I don't have any friends. Well, I have one. But he lives far, far away.

Lucy Tatty stepped forward and held up a little painting of Moo. 'He was her wish. When she was little she drew him, and when she went to the Karens she wished for him to be real.'

'But they twisted the wish. The twist was that I only had one friend, and that friend was Moo.'

Tiga looked at Felicity Bat, who tapped her watch. Tiga bit her lip and sat down on the fountain. 'Go on, Gloria.'

Felicity Bat threw her hands in the air. 'Good witches, ugh! Why?'

'I visit him sometimes, in their garden. But I make sure *never* to open up the Karens' line of communication

248

with the rest of Sinkville,' Gloria Tatty said. 'I tried to stop you getting involved, tried to take the book from you, but you ran away.'

'I knew it was you,' Felicity Bat whispered, staring at Gloria Tatty. 'I *am* a genius.'

'So how did you first discover the Karens?' Tiga asked.

Gloria Tatty took a seat on the edge of the fountain. 'Oh, I didn't discover them. I *invented* them.'

54

That Makes Sense ...

'So, wait,' Tiga said. 'You're telling us that you started writing a book called *The Karens*, about a coven of witches who lived in the Badlands.'

Gloria Tatty nodded. 'I was fascinated by what might be in the Badlands. No one ever went there.'

'Right,' Tiga went on. 'You put it on your shelf and then one day, when you were making a jam potion in a Crinkle Cauldron, something went wrong, there was a bang, everything fell from your bookshelf, including *The Karens* and the thirteen toads that lived in your kitchen.'

Gloria Tatty sighed. 'That is correct.'

'And somehow, the slightly skewed spell for jam and the Karens and the toads all combined to make the book real.'

'With the addition of the jelly castle,' Gloria Tatty explained. 'I didn't write that bit … must have something to do with the jam. So ridiculous! Who would put a jelly castle in a book?'

'So then what happened?' Tiga asked.

'Well,' Gloria Tatty said, shifting awkwardly on the fountain. 'I made my Moo wish, which of course they twisted. But before I knew they were bad news, I let some of my friends make wishes, too. Including Lucinda Bunch, who wanted to build a railway. She wished for the Sinkville Express – the most magical, majestic railway to ever make its way through the sky.

'Of course they twisted that too, and extended the track to go over the Badlands – a way of enticing witches to their jelly castle. Luckily, there were always horrible rumours of the Badlands and what might live there, so witches tended to jump off at Silver City or Driptown and go no further. Wait for it to come back around.'

'And does the railway always break because of Lucinda Bunch's wish?' Felicity Bat asked.

Gloria Tatty shook her head. 'No, that was because of a wish our friend Cathy made. She couldn't be bothered making her way up and down to the station, so she asked that they make it easier for her – she was thinking some private steps. But the Karens just bewitched a carriage to fall off the tracks instead. Technically, it was quicker for her to get off the Sinkville Express. They enjoy a twist … My friend Eddie wished she had the best shoe shop in Sinkville, so she got Shoes by Karen.'

'And the twist was they made her shoes like rockets!' Tiga cried. 'We saw an old lady wearing them.'

Gloria Tatty shook her head. 'No, her shoes were always like that. They changed her name to Karen. Every time she said Eddie, it came out as Karen. My friend Lucinda Bunch wasn't much worried about witches discovering the jelly castle, as they never went to the Badlands, but during her reign as Top Witch, evil Celia Crayfish closed down the railway anyway, as a way of isolating the cities, especially Silver City, where all the NAPA witches lived.

'Oh, I felt terrible for turning the toads into witches. I went along to a self-help group for witches who had done bad toad transformation spells. It was called TOAD TRANSFORMATION DISASTERS INC., but it was just witches who had turned people into toads, princes mainly, not the other way around! So I didn't mention the Karens, I just lied and said I was there to get inspiration for a book. I mean, who would turn a bunch of toads into troublemaking witches? This witch,' she said, pointing at herself. 'That's who.'

'It could happen to anyone,' Fluffanora lied.

'Lucinda Bunch decided to leave and go and live with the witches in the Coves. She told me to destroy the book and never speak of it again. But I worried if I destroyed it something bad might happen to Moo,' Gloria Tatty explained. 'So I hid it, behind the wall of the Silver Stacks bookshop. But then Tiga found the book and Fran made a wish.'

'I must say,' Gretal Green said, stepping in, 'while my daughter did find the book, I don't think she would've made a wish without being incredibly

suspicious of the Karens, and the only reason Fran made a wish was because I pushed her out of town with my little invented fairy Zarkle.'

'I FORGIVE YOU,' Fran said grandly, placing a finger on Gretal Green's shoulder.

'It's my fault for finding the book,' Tiga said.

'No, it's my fault for inventing Zarkle,' Gretal Green insisted.

'I AM TO BLAME!'

'Right, right, enough of this,' Felicity Bat said impatiently. 'For argument's sake, let's just say you're all to blame, yes?'

They turned and glared at her.

'What?' she said. 'This is one disaster you can't pin on me.'

Felicity Bat had a point. 'We have to turn the Karens back into toads – they're too dangerous.' Tiga paused; she didn't want to say it. 'If we destroy the Karens, we can't save Moo if he's a wish.'

Gloria Tatty hung her head. Lucy cuddled into her side.

'I understand,' Gloria Tatty said.

'*Finally*,' Felicity Bat said, completely inappropriately, before marching towards the Silver City train station. 'The train with Peggy on it should be here in a minute.'

55

Back to That Jelly Castle

'Oh, I hope this works,' Peggy said, as Tiga explained the plan to her in the carriage. Gretal Green and Fluffanora were in the carriage behind. Lucy Tatty had decided to stay at home with her gran, partly to be nice and partly because she was terrified of being trapped in a jelly castle again.

Every witch, each dressed up in her best gown and crammed into the Sinkville Express, was speaking at ear-splitting volume, shouting wishes, and delighting in the expected glory. Tiga wondered if maybe they'd have a rebellion on their hands afterwards, if they succeeded in destroying the jelly castle and no one got to make a wish.

The train rattled on into the barren land of the Badlands.

She looked behind her. Her mum was giving her the thumbs up. They were only moments away now. Tiga and Peggy had agreed to jump down first, as the train continued along on the track, in case the Karens came out of their castle and spotted Felicity Bat tampering with the pipe. They'd have to distract them.

'Oh, hello, Karens,' Peggy practised quietly. 'I've just come to tell you how much everyone in Ritzy liked the look of your Kake – and I'm not just distracting you because Felicity Bat is up there readying to pour hot Clutterbucks cocktail on your jelly castle.' She sighed. 'Why can't I lie?'

'Ready?' Tiga whispered, grabbing Peggy's hand.

And before they could say frogpuppets, they were falling fast towards the spongy softness of the jelly castle bridge. Tiga looked up just in time to see Felicity Bat fiddle with the pipe. *Not yet*, she thought as there was a whooshing sound. Tiga hit the jelly bridge, bouncing and biting her lip as she did so. 'OW!' she cried, grabbing frantically for Peggy's hand again.

'Got you!' Peggy said, as the pair of them bounced from the jelly bridge up and over into the jelly garden, just in time to see the glorious warm Clutterbucks cocktail thundering down from the pipes above.

'QUICK!' Tiga screamed, racing through the garden. The walls were high. How would they get out? They weren't meant to be trapped *in* the jelly castle when it melted! She could feel her boots slipping on the ground as the jelly began to soften. They rounded a corner, Peggy's hand shaking in hers.

Tiga heard Jelly-Horse Karen shouting, 'IT'S NOT

GOOD, DARLINGS! TO THE HORSES TO ESCAPE, DARLINGS!'

'THE HORSES! THAT'S IT!' Tiga cried, dragging Peggy around to the stables, where the two jelly horses stood looking concerned.

Tiga hastily mounted Cassidy, throwing herself so ambitiously over the horse's back, she nearly fell off the other side.

Peggy got on Sam, the other horse, backwards.

They galloped off around the grounds, watching as everything melted around them.

'SOMEONE'S NABBED THE HORSES!' echoed the voice of Cheese-Grater Karen, followed by Senior Karen shouting, 'NO, KAREN, DON'T YOU DARE SUGGEST SOMETHING INVOLVING THE CHEESE GRATER!'

Tiga spotted the fairies from the mirror and Caravan Conundrum. 'WHAT ABOUT THEM?' she shouted to Peggy.

'Oh, we're already dead, remember? *Expired*,' one shouted back.

'Right,' Tiga said, galloping on.

'We can't get trapped by the hot cocktail juice!' Peggy shouted. 'Also, let's not let these horses melt – I really like my one!'

Tiga stared at the gigantic jelly wall they were galloping towards. It had melted, but only slightly at the top. 'We need to jump the wall, Peggy!'

The Karens began to shrivel into toads.

'Darling! I'm toading, darling!'

'JELLY HORSES!' Fran squealed as she arrived on the scene. She grabbed the horses in midjump, coating them with glittery dust in her gigantic hands.

Tiga looked up at Fran adoringly; she was glad she'd caught them before they hit the other side – she was dreading the thud of the landing. Plus, Peggy was now hanging on to the horse's tail.

The large cake tower began to slip, falling fast into a deep, dark hole in the ground.

'Nooooo!' Senior Karen cried. 'NOT KAKES BY KAREN!'

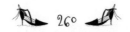

From the view high up on Fran, Tiga could see every-thing. The Karens scattering, half of them toads. Cloaks billowing. Senior Karen shouting. The turrets melting.

'We did it!' Tiga cheered as Felicity Bat levitated on to Fran's shoulder.

'You can't do this! I will stop you!' Senior Karen squealed, as she popped. And just like that, she was a harmless toad again.

'Wait a second,' shouted a witch in one of the carriages. 'Where have the Karens gone?'

A couple more witches peered over the edge.

'I CAN ONLY SEE TOADS.'

'The *toads* are granting wishes?'

'What?'

'Toads?' witches in the other carriages said, all nudging each other so they could get a better look.

'This is a load of frogwaffle!' a witch shouted. 'We've been had!'

Gretal Green cheered from the train, clattering along the track above them. It was directly over the jelly castle now.

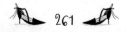

261

'WHAT IS GOING ON? CAN WE STILL MAKE WISHES WITHOUT THE JELLY CASTLE?' witches were shouting.

'NEVER TRUST A TOAD,' another witch shouted. 'RULE NUMBER ONE OF WISHING.'

Creak.

'Do you hear something?' Fluffanora said, but no one was listening.

'YOU DID IT, FEL-FEL!' Aggie Hoof cheered from beside Fluffanora.

'Wait,' Tiga said. 'Aggie Hoof's here? We didn't even tell her we were coming.'

'She's my *sidekick*,' Felicity Bat said proudly. 'She's like … hmm, what would be an above-the-pipes equivalent? She's like a bloodhound. Yes, a bloodhound. Always finds me.'

Creeeak.

'Do you hear something?' Fluffanora said.

'I hear you talking! And now I also hear myself talking,' Aggie Hoof said proudly.

Fluffanora sighed as their carriage gave one last

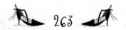

dramatic *CREAK* and came unstuck, hurtling towards the big hole the jelly turret had made in the ground below.

'NOOOOOOOOOO!' Tiga cried as she watched it fall. 'MUUUUUUM!'

Felicity Bat levitated fast towards it, grabbing hold of it. 'I'M NOT STRONG ENOUGH!' she shouted up to Tiga and Peggy, who could do nothing except look on in horror.

'HELP US!' the entire carriage yelled. 'SOMEONE HELP US!'

'FRAN!' Tiga shouted up to the oversized fairy. 'PUT US DOWN AND CATCH THAT CARRIAGE!'

Fran obliged, placing them gently on the ground, bounding over and cupping her hands above the gigantic hole. **'You know, Tiga, I'm excellent at catching. I once did a television programme about fairies catching things. It was called *Watch How Bad Fairies Are at Catching Things* … oh.'**

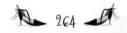

264

Tiga covered her eyes. *Please catch them, please catch them, please catch them*, she thought over and over again, as the screams got louder and closer. And then:

SILENCE.

Tiga didn't dare look. 'Did you – ?' she began.

'I DID A CATCH!' Fran cheered. Tiga opened her eyes to see Fran holding up the carriage and waving it about. She put it proudly on the ground.

'I DID A CATCH!'

And with an appropriately dusty bang that left everyone with glitter in their mouths, Fran morphed back to her normal fairy size.

She whipped out a mirror and looked at herself.

'Excuse me, fans, WHY DO I HAVE A JELLY HEDGE FOR HAIR?!'

Moo

As they were leaving, Tiga spotted something lying on the ground, in amongst all the goo of the melted jelly castle, and just to the left of the thirteen angry-looking toads.

She walked over and picked it up.

The lollipop from Moo's cart. She gently shook it, expecting the badly painted face to spring to life. But it didn't. She tucked it in her pocket.

'Come on Tiga, quickly!' Peggy yelled from the train. 'The track over the Badlands was a twist of one of their wishes and it's disappearing!' Parts of the track were glowing and fading, turning translucent in the dimming light.

Tiga looked up at the carriage and spotted the jelly

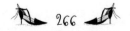

horses crammed in there, covered in Fran's glittery dust. 'How come the jelly horses are still all right?'

Peggy shrugged. 'Something to do with the fairy dust? I don't really know. Let's not question it too much.'

Tiga looked up at them and realised something. 'How did you all get back up there so quickly?' The one carriage that had dislodged was lying empty on the ground. Fluffanora and Tiga's mum and everyone else were sitting in another carriage now.

'The levitating one,' Peggy said, pointing to Felicity Bat, who was sweating and wheezing her way towards Tiga. 'Right,' she said breathlessly. 'Last one.'

RAILWAY WORKING AND FRAN WORKING ON LIFE STORY

The Sinkville Express isn't breaking every five minutes! All the carriages seem to be staying on the tracks rather than falling to the ground for absolutely no reason whatsoever. So take a trip on the Sinkville Express today!

In other news, Fran the Fabulous Fairy – once again fairy-sized – is making a film about her ordeal with famed Patricia the producer in Brollywood. Details of the film remain top secret, but our reporter went to ask Fran some questions at her caravan.

Reporter: Fran! It's me, the Ritzy City Post reporter. I just wanted to ask yo–

Our reporter was blasted with glittery dust and was too caked in it to finish – or start – the interview.

That Little Tube ...

'You did it, Tiga!' her mum said, twirling her around in the kitchen.

Tiga was relieved to be back to normal life – just some dinner, her mum, and an assortment of items of bewitched clothing called Dennis.

Fluffanora, Mrs Brew and Peggy were there too, while Felicity Bat took care of Linden House for the evening.

'Will Fran be joining us?' Gretal Green asked.

'I've missed her,' Mrs Brew said. 'Genuinely, even the screaming I LOVE YOU, MRS BREW.'

Tiga laughed and scooped a huge spoonful of jam from the jar. 'She's getting her beauty sleep. They start filming her new show tomorrow. Some real-life thing. I'm going to go and watch her rehearse in the morning.'

'Well, that's exciting,' Mrs Brew said, hugging Tiga's mum's arm. 'We should arrange a date to see it at the Silver Screen Cinema when it comes out.'

Lucy Tatty knocked on the kitchen window. 'Tiga, Peggy, Fluffanora! Come and play in the fountain! I HAVE SO MANY QUESTIONS ABOUT WITCH WARS!'

Tiga turned to her mum, who cackled. 'It's a Silver City tradition to play in the fountain. You must go, Tiga! Sometimes it opens up at the bottom and you're whooshed to this secret underwater village that's great fun.'

'Come in for dinner first,' Tiga said. Lucy gave her the thumbs up and came careering into the kitchen. She squealed and climbed on to the seat next to her. 'You're like the big sister I don't have yet. I'm obsessed with yooooou.'

'What do you mean that you don't have *yet*,' Fluffanora said. 'A big sister would be older than you, so you'd have her already.'

'Oh yeah!' Lucy Tatty said. 'I forgot they have to be

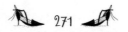

271

older. I always just think it's taller. Oh, Tiga,' she said, handing her Gloria Tatty's drawing of Moo. 'My gran wanted you to have this.'

Peggy rolled a large map out on the table. 'That reminds me! I'm going to build in the Badlands. Have all sorts of houses and things there! And thirteen toads, of course.'

'Can they cause trouble as toads, the Karens?' Gretal Green asked.

Peggy shook her head. 'They can't even speak. Oh, and there will be two very cool jelly horses, covered in Fran's dust.'

'They're still covered in glittery dust?' Fluffanora asked.

'I'm afraid they'll melt if I remove it,' Peggy explained.

'Well, quite,' Mrs Brew said.

'And guess what I'm going to call the place?'

'The Badlands?' Fluffanora guessed.

'No, no!' Peggy said, laughing. 'Lucy, you'll like this. I'm going to call it Glormoo!'

They all stared at her.

'You know … because Gloria and Moo … Glormoo?'

'Eh, yeah, well,' they all muttered awkwardly at once.

Fluffanora placed a hand on Peggy's arm. 'I'm sure once you have a nice sign up for it, it'll sound better.'

'It sounds good, I thought. You know, just off on holiday to ride jelly horses in Glormoo. You can't beat a day in Glormoo,' Peggy mumbled to herself.

'What about Tatty Moor?' Tiga suggested. 'It sounds less … weird?'

'Yes,' Peggy said slowly. 'I like it. And we can have a grand hotel there called Glormoo! Yes, Glormoo Castle.'

'Look at you, being all fancy,' Fluffanora said, flashing Peggy a smile. 'Building *castles*.'

Tiga watched as her mum turned and lifted a small test tube from the kitchen counter. She stared at it for a moment and then shook her head. With a flick of a finger, she sent it sailing towards the bin.

Tiga gulped down some jam and leapt in the air to grab it.

'You're going to get rid of it? I thought it was one of your best inventions!'

'It only causes trouble,' Gretal Green said. 'I don't think I'll be making more fairies any time soon. At least not while Fran is around.'

'I suppose. Fran is very sensitive,' Tiga said. She was starting to love all the weird and wonderful inventions and didn't want her mum to feel she couldn't experiment. Tiga clutched the test tube tighter. She stared down at the picture of Moo, running her hand over it. She remembered the little wooden lollipop she'd brought back from the Badlands. 'Wait,' she said, grinning. 'Do you think we could make one more small thing?'

58

Fluff My Hair and Call Me Maggots

On the set of Fran's new film, witches were putting the finishing touches to the miniature model of Ritzy City. It was perfect, with immaculate detail – everything from the little lamp posts and flowerpots to the tiny shop signs.

Tiga sat on a director's chair in the corner giving Fran the thumbs up.

'Now, Fran, if you could just squash that model of the Brew's fashion boutique with your shoe and scream "AAAARGH!" that would be great.'

Fran held a hand in the air, looking horrified. '*Patricia the producer*, I would *never* squash Brew's.'

'All righty, let's move on to your next line, when you run around bellowing through your gigantic mouth ...'

'Die, witches, die,' Fran said, reading the script slowly. She placed it on the ground and looked at Patricia the producer. 'This isn't a true-life story at all, is it? YOU'RE MAKING A HORROR FILM OUT OF MY ORDEAL!'

Patricia and Crispy looked guiltily at their shoes. 'But we've made a replica Karen toad and a squidgy pony with state-of-the-art fake jelly,' Patricia the producer tried.

'Well, I will not be a part of this! I would never do a horror. Crispy tried to get me in her *Toe Pinchers* film and I said absolutely not! Not even if I get to play all the parts.'

'That would be impossible, to play all the parts,' Crispy said quietly, but Fran was on a roll.

'And *another* thing. I am the best fairy actress in all of Sinkville, have we all forgotten that? Who else holds the award for Best and Only Fairy Film of the Year? No one, because I am still quite literally holding it!'

She held it up and waved it about.

'My film *Toe Pinchers* won the award for Special

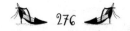

Effects That You Could Do Yourself at Home,' Crispy said proudly.

'CRISPY, THAT IS NOT A GOOD THING,' Fran scoffed, floating towards the door.

Patricia the producer coughed. 'We think it'll win more awards if it's a horror.'

Fran paused. 'Awards? More than one?'

Patricia the producer nodded.

'Well, Patricia, fluff my hair and call me Maggots! I'll DO IT.'

Tiga smiled. Sinkville was finally back to *normal*.

Fran's jelly hair wobbled as she bounded across the set.

Well, almost.

Look out for

Bad Mermaids

A new series by Sibéal Pounder

March 2017